"You're sure you want this...me?"

The words thrilled Emily, raising a rash of goose bumps across her skin, making her quiver and then tense as she felt Matt's lips tracing the shape of her mouth. Her tension died in a flood of wonder and pleasure.

Why had she never known that it was possible to feel like this? To know that the delicate, almost hesitant touch of another mouth against her own could arouse her to such dizzying pleasure and need?

It was as though this unusual exploratory meeting of their lips was something she had dreamed of for an aeon of time, rather than realizing she wanted his touch only seconds before experiencing it.

Against Matt's mouth, she whispered back, "Yes...I want you."

PENNY JORDAN was constantly in trouble in school because of her inability to stop daydreaming—especially during French lessons. In her teens, she was an avid romance reader, although it didn't occur to her to try writing one herself until she was older. "My first half dozen attempts ended up ingloriously," she remembers, "but I persevered, and one manuscript was finished." She plucked up the courage to send it to a publisher, convinced her book would be rejected. It wasn't, and the rest is history! Penny is married and lives in Cheshire.

Penny Jordan's striking mainstream novel *Power Play* quickly became a *New York Times* bestseller. She followed that success with *Silver*, a story of ambition, passion and intrigue. Her latest blockbuster, *The Hidden Years*, lays bare the choices all women face in their search for love.

Books by Penny Jordan

HARLEQUIN PRESENTS
1339—TIME FOR TRUST
1353—SO CLOSE AND NO CLOSER
1369—BITTER BETRAYAL
1388—BREAKING AWAY
1404—UNSPOKEN DESIRE
1418—RIVAL ATTRACTIONS

HARLEQUIN SIGNATURE EDITION
LOVE'S CHOICES
STRONGER THAN YEARNING

PENNY JORDAN

out of the night

Harlequin Books

TORONTO • NEW YORK • LONDON
AMSTERDAM • PARIS • SYDNEY • HAMBURG
STOCKHOLM • ATHENS • TOKYO • MILAN

Harlequin Presents first edition January 1992
ISBN 0-373-11427-3

Original hardcover edition published in 1990
by Mills & Boon Limited

OUT OF THE NIGHT

CHAPTER ONE

EMILY frowned as the flurries of snow ominously started to thicken into what her lifelong experience of these border hills told her threatened to be a fully grown blizzard.

She was no fool—no town-bred child whose only real experience of the truly life-threatening danger of heavy snows on these hills came from watching televised newsreel film.

Perhaps she ought to have put off her departure, but she had already spent two days longer with her parents than she had intended and, as she had explained to them, Uncle John had reached a critical point with his book and would be champing at the bit to get working on it, so she couldn't really delay any longer.

She had seen the wry, almost amused looks her parents had exchanged, and, even though she'd thought she had taught herself long ago to accept herself as she was, she had felt a sharp, painful flash of hurt, reminding her of her childhood.

Perhaps it had been because Gracie had also been at home. Gracie: four years her junior, pretty, ambitious, self-confident, popular with everyone who knew her, and now engaged to be married to the tall and obviously besotted Australian she had brought home with her.

Emily knew that her parents were baffled by her; she could imagine them wondering where she had come from, their quiet, introverted, almost prim little brown wren of an eldest child—her smallness somehow all the more noticeable in a family of tall Scandinavian-type blondes.

And she was different in other ways, too. She had been conceived while her parents were walking in the Andes; although their home base was here in the border hills, her parents were intrepid adventurers, forever off to far-flung parts of the globe. Her father had the family talent with words and wrote very clever and witty travel books, wonderfully illustrated by her mother. Gracie, too, was a traveller, loving nothing more than to take off for far-away places at a moment's notice.

Emily, though, was different—she hated travelling, and she hated adventuring even more. She was the quiet, stay-at-home type. She knew she puzzled and sometimes disappointed her parents. They loved her, she knew that, but it was a love fraught with a lack of true understanding of her nature.

After she had left university, they had talked enthusiastically and encouragingly of her taking a year off to travel the world, and had been rather like two hurt children when she had told them that that was the last thing she had wanted to do.

When they had learned that she was going to work for her father's uncle, an academic who had devoted his life to the mysteries of ancient Egyptian civilisation, they had been astounded. Bury herself in the quiet backwater close to Oxford where Uncle John held the Chair in Ancient Civilisations in one of the colleges? They hadn't been able to understand her decision then, and she knew that they understood it even less now, four years later.

Once it had hurt her knowing that they had probably dismissed her as dull and boring, because she *did* have her dreams and her hopes... dreams and hopes that were far removed from those of her parents and sister. Unlike them she had no craving for travel, no thirst for fresh sights and unfamiliar pastures—her dreams did not have wide horizons. It was the small, intimate world of domestic happiness she craved: a home, husband, children—love that could be shared.

Unfashionable dreams, these days; dreams that she was afraid to voice, knowing how they would be received even by her parents. Once she had even thought they might come true.

She had met Gerry while she was at university, and for the first time in her life she had been able to step outside the confines of her lack of self-confidence... her feeling that, in being the way she was, she had somehow let both her parents and herself down. With Gerry she had felt different: self-confident, attractive, interesting. He had courted her and flattered her, wooing her skilfully and ardently, but not too ardently that she took fright.

And then, just when she had been happily beginning to dream about engagement rings and weddings, the cruel revelation of the truth had come. Gerry hadn't loved her at all. She had been the victim of a particularly nasty and cruel male joke.

It had happened the weekend after she had gone home to see her parents. Gerry had come round to see her on the Monday. He had kissed her passionately...so passionately that she had been a little afraid.

Sex had been something new and untried for her and, much as she had adored Gerry, his obvious experience and expertise had seemed to underline her own lack of them, making her hesitant to allow the feelings inside her to break through the barriers she had imposed on them.

Normally so patient and understanding with her, this time Gerry had lost his temper. What did she want, he had asked her nastily—to remain a virgin all her life? Before she could speak he had gone on to tell her cruelly that she was lucky he was prepared to overlook her ignorance of sex, her inability to turn him on, her total lack of any kind of knowledge about how to make herself desirable.

She had never seen him in a temper before, and she had shrunk from the uncontrollable anger emanating from him, her face tense and white as she had listened in disbelief to what he had been saying.

Her lack of response had only seemed to goad him on. 'Look at you,' he had derided. 'Did you really think I could possibly want *you*? Do you really imagine I'm going to all this trouble simply so that I can take your frigid body to bed? No way...'

He had stopped then, conscious that he had said too much, but it had already been too late. Feeling as though her world had broken apart in front of her, Emily had forced herself to confront the truth and to demand to know what he had meant.

Watching him hesitate, knowing how much she ached to believe the lies she already knew he was trying to formulate, she had deliberately denied herself that surcease, and had said quietly, 'Will it help you to tell me the truth if I say that there's absolutely no chance of our being lovers?'

If she had thought his temper was out of control before, she had then realised her mistake. The language he'd used, the virulence of his temper, ought to have terrified her; but somehow she had gone beyond that, to find a temporary harbour in some small corner of her mind that had sheltered her while she had listened to him pouring scorn on her, telling her that the only reason he had bothered with her was because some fellow students had challenged him to get her into bed—humiliatingly having guessed at her total lack of experience. Heavy bets had been placed on his ability to do so. He himself had stood to gain financially if he succeeded.

And what had shocked her most of all was that he had not been in the least ashamed of admitting it to her. If anything, he had seemed to think that she was the one who had behaved badly—that she had been the one at fault. Well, perhaps she had been, although her fault had not been in not allowing him to use her body, but in ever thinking that he might have actually cared for her.

She had seen him so clearly then, and had hated herself for the tawdry cheapness of the image she had foolishly believed she had loved. What she had loved was a man she had created out of her own daydreams and imagination and then clothed with Gerry's features. The real Gerry had been nothing like the man of her daydreams.

She had learned a hard and painful lesson, and she had sworn to herself, as she had quietly demanded to know exactly how much money he would have won had he succeeded, that never again would she repeat her folly. When he had grudgingly told her, she had written out a cheque and had handed it to him.

Her parents had been generous, and she had never been short of money. There had been very little she had wanted to spend it on. She had not been fashion-conscious like most of her contemporaries. She had smiled grimly to herself, realising that she was probably the only girl in the whole university who still wore clothes that approximated to something like a school uniform: neat woollen jumpers, sturdy brogues. She dressed for comfort in clothes that helped her to blend in with her surroundings, not stand out from them.

Gerry had taken the cheque, blustering that it was no less than she owed him, and adding sneeringly that if she changed her mind and decided that she wanted to get rid of her virginity after all, he'd be prepared to oblige her for a similar amount. 'After all,' he had taunted her, 'what's the point in saving it ... unless you're planning to become a nun ...'

She would cry later, she had told herself stonily, watching him leave. She would grieve later for the destruction of her dreams, but right now the most important thing focusing her mind had been that somehow or other she patch together the broken shards of what had once been a person named Emily Francine Blacklaw, and that she find a way of making that person appear to be a human being, and not a robot from whom the ability to think, reason and feel had been taken away.

Somehow, from a reserve of strength buried inside her which she hadn't known she possessed, she had managed it, just as she had managed to appear not to notice the sometimes curious, sometimes amused looks of those of her peers who must have been privy to the original bet.

It had been the year of her finals, but now, instead of looking forward to the future, she had simply tried to endure the passing of each day as best she could. Then in a letter from her mother had come the news that her father's Uncle John had been about to embark on actually getting down to write the book he had been threatening to work on for as long as Emily could remember. He would need to find a devoted and very patient research-assistant-cum-secretary, her mother had written, and, when she had read those words, Emily had known that she had found somewhere where she could hide herself away from a world which had become too painful and alien for her. Not a convent, precisely, she had thought with the small bitter smile which had been beginning to replace her once warm and natural, if slightly shy beam.

Perhaps if her parents hadn't been so busy with the preparations for their forthcoming trip to Mexico...perhaps if her sister hadn't elected to take a year off between A levels and university and travel to Australia...perhaps if she had had a close girl-friend to note the warning signs and do something about them, someone might have intervened and turned her back to face the world instead of withdrawing from it. But fate had decreed otherwise, and, by the time her parents had returned from

Mexico, she had obtained her degree and had been working for Uncle John for three months.

Despite the almost monastic life he lived in the rather ramshackle house several miles outside the university town, Emily had settled very well into her new existence. She enjoyed working for Uncle John, and she had the patience to help him to disentangle and transcribe the notebooks which held over twenty years of notes made supposedly in preparation for the opus it had been his life's dream to complete.

Although neither of them realised it, Emily's was the hand and brain that had translated the dusty dry facts so painstakingly uncovered by the scholar into the first outline for a book—a book which John Blacklaw's publishers had found surprisingly readable. They were an old-established and very small firm, based in the same town as the university, and well versed in dealing with their sometimes eccentric would-be authors.

Peter Cavendish, the great-great-grandson of the original founder of the business, had raised a few tut-tuts from his older relatives when he had commented enthusiastically that at last he had read a manuscript which he could not only understand, but which he had also found made him want to explore its subject in more detail.

Peter Cavendish was thirty years old and unmarried and, in the eyes of his grandfather and great-uncles, a little too frivolous for their kind of publishing. Privately, Peter confided to his mother and sisters that he intended to drag the firm into the twenty-first century by the scruff of its neck if necessary. 'And I think I've found the book which will do it...'

Neither Emily nor Uncle John were as yet aware of his intentions; the book was still in its very early stages, and he had enough of the family caution to want to make sure that the old boy could produce more than half a dozen chapters before committing himself.

Now, as she drove with proper respect for the howling wind buffeting the car and the thick snow which was all too quickly whitening the road, Emily wished she had ignored Gracie's pleas to her to extend her visit long enough for her to get to know Travis, her Australian fiancé; but, ever sensitive to the opinions of others, Emily had felt that if she did not stay her family might think that it was because she was envious or resentful of Gracie's happiness.

She had once overheard her mother discussing her with her father, saying that she was the type of girl best suited to marriage with a similarly quiet man, with whom she could live in suburban security to raise the requisite two-point-odd children. The words hadn't meant to be hurtful, but they had been to a girl on the threshold of womanhood who had still been dreaming of a lover of heroic proportions... a lover straight from one of Sir Walter Scott's novels, or one of Georgette Heyer's wondrous Regency Romances; a lover who would see through her quiet exterior, who would cherish and adore her...

She knew better now, and, if it was foolish of her to say to herself that, if she could not reach the stars, if she could not experience the heights of emotional intensity she had once dreamed of reaching, then she would rather not bother than settle for the kind of mundane relationship her mother had described, then only she knew of that folly.

And so she had stayed on, to smile at Gracie's Travis, and to hide her real feelings at the astonishment on his face as he had looked from the tall, golden, glowing Blacklaw parents and his equally golden, glowing fiancée to the small, brown little creature who was their daughter and sister.

And then yesterday it had snowed enough for Gracie to insist on their digging out the old sledge and going tobogganing on the snowy fields beyond the house. Unwillingly, Emily had allowed herself to be dragged along with them. And of course it should be her luck that, instead of sledging skilfully to the bottom of the hill, she should have hit a covered root and end up soaking wet and bruised sitting in a shallow, muddy pool of water hiding beneath the ice.

What had made it even more unfortunate was that she had not brought a second skirt with her, having only intended to stay two days; and so now, instead of travelling home in her neat pleated skirt and sensible blouse and jumper, she was wearing what Gracie had described as a 'sweatshirt' in a shade of fuchsia pink which might suit Gracie but which she felt was hideously startling on her—and worse still there was a rather dubious slogan printed across its chest in two-inch-high letters.

To go with this, Gracie had proffered a pair of jeans, ruthlessly ignoring Emily's protests that they were far too tight and too long, telling her that she could easily shorten them, and then immediately doing so, so that Emily had had no option but to put the things on and to leave the soaking wet skirt behind her.

Weakly she had also accepted the multicoloured and huge sweater Travis had pressed on her as a 'present'. Gracie had plainly not told him what Emily looked like, because the sweater had obviously been designed for a woman like her sister— someone tall and self-confident enough to carry off such a very vivid and eye-catching item.

In fact, the only things she had on that were her own, apart from her underwear, were her sensible flat shoes; but, looking at them and then looking at the frighteningly fast-thickening snow, Emily was forced to acknowledge that a sturdy pair of wellington boots was likely to have been more use to her.

She had deliberately chosen to drive back to Oxford over one of the high passes to avoid the traffic. Her father, who always listened to the farming weather, had warned her that more snow had been forecast, but she had assumed that he meant further small flurries of the sort they had had over the previous two days—not this potentially life-threatening blizzard. However, there was no point in panicking. A quick glance in her rearview mirror confirmed her opinion that she had come too far up the pass to turn back; another half-hour and she would be over the pass and down the other side, heading for the small village of Thraxton, whereas if she turned back she would have to drive for over an hour to reach the nearest town.

She frowned again as she felt her car wheels start to spin, and slowed down to a safe crawl, thanking providence that her mother's housekeeper, Louise, had insisted on providing her with a huge flask of coffee and some sandwiches. She had a new unread paperback in her overnight case, plus the car rug she always carried with her to tuck round Uncle John's knees. He suffered badly from arthritis now, and welcomed such small touches of extra warmth and cosseting.

If she did have to spend the night in the car, she would survive. It wouldn't be pleasant, of course, but she was sensible enough to know that it would be far wiser for her to stay in her car than to risk exposure by getting out and going looking for help. Not that she was likely to find any. These hills were barren and uninhabited, and it was too late now to wish that she had chosen the more sensible busy route.

Although it was dark, the whiteness of the snow-covered landscape gave off an eerie light; her eyes, straining to see through the driving snow clogging the windscreen-wipers, were beginning to ache, and she was conscious of how much her car was slipping and sliding despite her low gear... How much further before she reached the highest point of the road? She tried to remember if she was right in thinking there was a small lay-by not far ahead, and whether it would be more sensible to pull in there or risk going on.

She hadn't seen any other cars since it started to snow. Soon, with the wind, the snow would start to drift. If that happened and her car got covered... She bit her lip, telling herself stoically that nothing could be gained from letting her imagination panic her—and then, just when she was beginning to think she might make it, the car skidded violently, out of control, and plunged off the road and down into a deep snow-filled ditch.

She bumped her head as the car came to rest, the seatbelt jerking her backwards painfully, and as she moved cautiously, unfastening it and forcing open her door, she was thankful to discover that she had no real injuries.

As she climbed out of the car and into the snow and surveyed them both rather shakily, she was forced to admit what she had already known: that the only way her car was going to get out of the ditch was by being lifted out. Even with the spade she had in the boot, it would be impossible for her to dig herself out.

Biting her lip with irritation, she acknowledged that there was nothing else for it. She would have to spend the night in the car and hope that by morning the snow had gone and that she would be able to appeal to a fellow motorist for help.

She was just about to get back inside the car when, almost like a miracle, she heard the sound of another car approaching. Instinctively she stepped out into the road to attract the driver's attention, only realising too late that the sight of her was likely to make them brake and suffer the same fate as herself.

The driver of the battered, long-wheelbase, four-wheel-drive vehicle that swung round the bend obviously thought the same thing, because he glared at her and mouthed something she suspected was far from complimentary—but he did at least stop.

Although, when she saw him climbing out of his vehicle, she wondered whether that was a good thing or not. He was huge: well over six feet with shoulders to match, his features concealed by a tousled mop of black hair and an equally unprepossessing beard.

As he came towards her Emily saw that he was glowering at her. He paused frowningly a foot away from her, wiping the snow off his face with a hand that she saw was hard and scarred as though he worked outdoors a lot, and she wondered if he was a local farmer.

'Just what in hell are you trying to do? Kill us both?' The sharp, incisive words were not spoken with a local accent or with any kind of accent at all, Emily recognised as she assimilated his angry criticism. It had perhaps been foolish of her to stand in the road, but his anger was surely a little excessive?

'You young kids, you're all the same,' he continued, still glowering. 'Not a scrap of sense in your heads...'

Emily stared at him. Just how old did he think she was? Despite his grim appearance, she doubted that he was much more than in his early thirties; she was twenty-six—not a lot of difference, and certainly not sufficient to merit his attitude.

'Now, just a minute——' she began, but he immediately cut across what she had been going to say, demanding curtly, 'Have you any idea of how easy it would be for you to freeze to death out here? Look at you, dressed in an outfit more suitable for a...a city disco than these winter hills. Have you any idea just what's involved in mounting rescue services for idiots like you? Just what it costs in men's time? The rescue services in these hills are run by volunteers, men already badly pressed for time—men who willingly risk their lives for idiots like you with no more sense than to go driving in weather when any sane person wouldn't set a foot out of doors...'

Emily listened to him in growing resentment. Just what kind of person did he think she was? The answer was simple. He thought she was some kind of irresponsible, idiotic teenager. Dressed for a disco, indeed. She winced a little, recollecting her own reluctance to don the sweatshirt Gracie had proffered, and wondered what on earth this large angry man would make of Travis's many-hued jumper—and then decided that it was perhaps as well she would never know.

As for that remark about the rescue services— her own father was one of those volunteers, and she knew all about the hazards they had to face.

Before she could say as much the man was talking again, gesturing towards her car with evident disgust as he said bluntly, 'Well, you've no chance of getting that thing back on the road without a pick-up. By rights I ought to leave you here to give you a taste of what happens to idiots like you when they ignore the warnings of far more sensible human beings, and go out for drives in blizzard weather conditions; but, as you're all too likely to ignore any advice I might give you about staying put in your car and wander off somewhere causing God alone knows what sort of trouble for whoever has to find you, I suppose I'd better give you a lift.'

A little to her own astonishment, Emily found that she was actually grinding her teeth. She had always considered herself to be a very even-tempered human being; even in the face of Gerry's cruelty she had remained calm—on the surface at least—but suddenly she was discovering how wrong she had been about herself, and how very satisfactory it would be to fling his arrogant and grudging offer of help right back in his face.

Maturity won out over inclination, though. She had no wish to spend the night in her car...not with the intensity of the blizzard-driven snowstorm increasing with every second that passed...not when she could see for herself that already the snow was drifting and that, if it continued to do so, it might be several days and not several hours before she was rescued from her trapped car.

And so, biting back her ire, she said as coldly as she could, 'I'll just get my things from the car.'

Behind her she heard a derisive snort as he muttered under his breath, 'God, you females... You can't go anywhere without half a ton of make-up...'

Make-up... A strong desire to giggle overwhelmed her. Her make-up was restricted to moisturiser, blusher, soft pink lipstick, mascara and the merest touch of eyeshadow, and only those because she had grown tired of her mother's and Gracie's reproaches that she didn't make enough of herself. No—what she wanted from her car was the warmth of Travis's sweater, the rug, and the thermos flask of coffee and the sandwiches Louise had given her.

As she ploughed her way back to her car through snow which had deepened dramatically in the time she had been standing on the road, she pushed her hair off her face, grimacing a little. She had been so busy working with Uncle John that she hadn't had time for her normal bimonthly trim of the neat bob in which she normally wore her hair. The result was that it had grown down to her shoulders and constantly swung down over her face in a most irritating fashion. Her mother had said that she liked it longer; Gracie had raised her eyebrows and announced that it made her look even more ethereally fragile than usual. Emily thought it was just plain untidy.

She collected her things from her car with efficient ease and saw her unwilling rescuer's expression change as she returned towards him, carrying the thermos flask and blanket.

'Typical student,' he grunted critically. 'Planning to sleep in your car, I suppose...'

Emily opened her mouth to deny that she had been intending to do any such thing, and to set him right about the other facts he had got completely wrong, and then closed it again as he continued brusquely, 'I suppose we'd better introduce ourselves as we're going to be travelling companions. I'm Matthew Slater. Most people call me Matt.'

Later she had no idea what on earth made her say it...what rash folly had prompted the impulse that had her replying, not by introducing herself as Emily Blacklaw, but simply as Francine.

'Francine.' She saw the way his eyebrows rose and added sweetly, 'It's a family name.'

She thought she heard him say under his breath, 'It would have to be,' but he had his back to her and was already ploughing his way back to his vehicle.

Automatically following in his footsteps, Emily discovered how very much longer his stride was than her own, but her jeans were already soaking wet from the knees down, and anything that saved her from sinking knee-deep in a fresh coating of snow was worth a little effort.

He made no attempt to relieve her of her possessions, nor to help her in any way at all, she fumed as she struggled against the blizzard buffeting her body and the snow stinging her face. Only when she reached the safety of his vehicle did he offer a helping hand, and then only a grim inspection of her snow-covered frame and the height from the ground to the passenger door.

She supposed that she ought not to have been surprised at the ease with which he picked her up and virtually dumped her on the passenger seat. She was after all only small and slight, and he was extremely large, but there was something so disconcertingly unfamiliar about the sensation of male hands grasping her body... about the scent of male skin dominating even the cold smell of the snow... about the warmth of male breath grazing her skin that, all of a sudden, she felt acutely breathless and helpless.

'Where were you going, anyway?' he asked her as he climbed in beside her and relieved her of her possessions, putting them casually in the rear of the vehicle.

It was, Emily now recognised, equipped for rugged terrain, and the pack on the floor behind her looked as though it belonged to a climber or walker. The rear passenger seats had been removed to make room for extra equipment, or perhaps for carrying stock rather than people.

'Oh, to meet some boyfriend, I suppose. Well, if he's any sense he'll have stayed at home. Women...'

He obviously didn't have a very high opinion of her sex, Emily realised warily.

'I can drop you off in Thraxton,' he told her as he closed his door and started the engine.

From there she could ring her parents and organise a garage to pick up her car. She could travel south by train... her mind busy with the arrangements she had to make, she was glad of her companion's silence as he concentrated on his driving.

His four-wheel-drive vehicle had a very powerful heater. She stretched her toes out towards its warmth, wishing it were possible to remove her soaking wet clammy jeans. The sound of the windscreen-wipers was rhythmic and lulling.

Her eyes ached still from the strain of staring through her own windscreen. Drowsily she mused on how odd it was that she should feel so safe and relaxed with this brusque stranger. Normally she found strange men intimidating, and was sensitive to how she must appear in their eyes, to how they must contrast her lack of looks and sexuality to other women they knew—a sensitivity born of Gerry's cruelty to her and her subsequent total loss of confidence in herself as a woman. This man had made his uncomplimentary view of her sex so plain, she felt none of her normal constraint. It still amazed her that he should have mistaken her for a giddy teenager prepared to drive miles through a blizzard to go dancing with a supposed boyfriend.

Perhaps she rather liked that false image of herself, she wondered sleepily... perhaps that was why she had given him her second name, instead of her workaday and, to her eyes, very applicable first name. Emily... It suited her, so everyone said. So why was it when this man looked at her he hadn't seen an Emily but instead had mistaken her for a Francine? She was still sleepily musing over this conundrum when she fell asleep.

The man at her side gave her a frowning look of disapproval and then returned his concentration to his driving.

It had been a mistake to delay his departure from the Cairngorms for that extra day. He had an appointment tomorrow that he must keep, but this was likely to be his last opportunity to go climbing for quite some time. Still, he was paying for his self-indulgence now, having to help out this idiotic female... He grimaced as he looked at her. Tiny little thing... what on earth had possessed her to wear that appalling garment with its dubious invitation? She looked so young and innocent as she slept. His mouth tightened. As he had good cause to know, her sex was adept at promoting fictitious images. He had once thought Jolie just as innocent—until he had found her in bed with someone else three days before their wedding.

She had cried and pleaded with him, begged him to understand, and he, God help him, had been tempted... until he had discovered the real reason she had wanted to marry him. Being wanted for your wealth was one of the penalties paid by the offspring of rich men, his father had told him, adding forthrightly that in any case he considered twenty-one far too young for a man to marry. He had had a miraculous escape, he had added.

Perhaps he had...certainly the experience had soured him against committing himself to any kind of permanent relationship with someone else. There had been women, of course—episodes he was not proud of and which soon lost their savour—but over these last few years there had been no one, and he had been content with that state of affairs. Until now, because for some reason this idiotic female asleep beside him was making him uncomfortably aware of the fact that he was, after all, a man and not a monk!

He wondered how old she was...eighteen? Nineteen? He was thirty-four, and she was not his type anyway. Jolie had been a *soignée* elegant blonde, tall and slim. This...this child wasn't much over five feet two, and as for her shape—impossible to see what it was like under that appalling sweatshirt.

When he had picked her up, though, his hands had fitted easily around her waist. Her wrists were fragile and narrow, and she had the longest eyelashes he had ever seen—unless they were false...

As he stole another look at Emily's sleeping profile, just to make sure that he hadn't imagined that thick, long sweep of curling lashes, the road dipped for a hundred-yard stretch where it was fully exposed to the full force of the blizzard, and before he could do a single thing about it his Land Rover had run straight into an eight-foot drift of snow.

CHAPTER TWO

IT WAS Matt's savage curse that woke Emily, combined with the sudden jarring sensation as the Land Rover's engine stalled.

As she opened her eyes and blinked sleepily, she realised immediately what had happened, and it was Emily and not Francine who asked automatically, 'Can we dig our way out, or...?'

Matt gave her a sharp look. Was she serious? The only women he knew would rather die of exposure than risk their long varnished nails by wielding a spade. 'It might be easier to reverse; the drifts are only going to get worse if we turn back.'

Immediately Emily shook her head. 'It's too late,' she told him calmly. 'The road will be blocked where it dips down to the river. That's always the first place the drifts form.'

He gave her another sharp look, but recalling the stretch of road she was referring to had to admit that she was probably right.

'It looks as if we're well and truly stuck, then,' he said tersely. Inwardly he was cursing himself for not setting out earlier. If he had not been having doubts about the wisdom of interviewing for this new job...

Now he had no option but to spend what was left of the night in the close confines of his Land Rover with this idiotic female, who smelled dis-

26

turbingly of some kind of no doubt expensive French scent.

Emily would have been stunned had she known what he was thinking. The French scent was in fact the rose-scented soap she always used and was so accustomed to that she had no idea of the way it clung so pervasively to her skin.

'I suppose we ought to get out and check that we *can't* dig our way out,' she suggested cautiously.

'I'll do it,' her companion said tersely. 'There's no point in both of us getting soaked.'

Emily wanted to point out that, since *she* already was, it seemed sensible that she should be the one to check on the extent of the drifting; but she suspected that this arrogant, lordly male would never accept that a woman could do such a task as effectively as a man, so she said nothing and watched as he opened his door and climbed out.

His inspection of their plight was thorough, she had to admit when he eventually returned. She doubted that she would have had the fortitude to stay outside for so long. Snow clung to his sweater and jeans, turning him into a walking snowman, and she watched as he brushed the worst of it off before climbing back inside.

'We haven't a hope of getting out,' he told her crisply, 'and God knows how long we'll be stuck here for.'

'Probably only until tomorrow,' Emily told him. 'They normally try to keep this road open if they can. It's a pity we can't pull off the road to leave room for the snow plough,' she added thoughtfully, causing him to give her a considering look.

Perhaps, after all, she was not as idiotic as he had first assumed; certainly there was no trace of panic in her behaviour at his announcement that they were stuck. He wished grimly now that he had stopped at that garage and bought himself something to eat, but he had been so conscious of how late he had been in leaving.

'I suppose we'd better keep the coffee until we get cold,' Emily murmured, speaking her thoughts out loud as she sifted through her brain trying to remember the most important laws of cold-weather survival.

They were more fortunate than most. They had warm clothing, a hot drink, some food, and a certain amount of shelter, although she suspected that the Land Rover would soon become very cold indeed without the engine running. She glanced over her shoulder into the rear of the vehicle, wondering if she had actually seen what looked like a rolled up sleeping-bag there. If so, they were very fortunate indeed. If not... well, she had Travis's sweater to give her an extra layer of warmth, and, if only she could pluck up the courage to do so, she really ought to remove her wet jeans and wrap the car rug round her legs. It was silly to worry about modesty in this kind of situation, where the cold, wet fabric wrapped around her legs could dangerously lower her body temperature to the point where at some stage during their incarceration she could start to suffer from hypothermia.

As though he had read her mind, Matt suddenly said curtly, 'You'd better get those wet jeans off. I've got a spare pair you can have.'

Emily struggled not to laugh at the thought of her wearing his jeans. 'That won't be necessary,' she told him coolly. 'I can use the car rug.'

To her astonishment he shook his head. 'No, we'll both need that later.'

When he saw her expression he said grimly, 'Look, *I* don't like this any more than you, but we've got to face facts. The temperature in here is going to drop so fast that within an hour both of us are going to be frozen. That means we've got to preserve what body heat we still have by any means we can.' He glanced at his watch. 'It's almost nine o'clock. A bit early to be thinking of going to sleep, but in the circumstances it's going to be our wisest course of action. I've got a sleeping-bag in the back. It's large enough for both of us.'

He heard her automatic protest and frowned at her before saying stiffly, 'Spare me the shrieks of maidenly modesty; this isn't some kind of sexual come-on. I'd be saying exactly the same thing to another man, and, given the choice between a man, a woman or a dog to share the sleeping-bag with me right now, I'd prefer the dog.'

Emily was quite sure that he would, and she knew what he was saying was the only sensible course of action open to them. Even so, something vulnerable and tender inside her shrank from the intimacy of what she knew must be done. To sleep so physically closely to this hard, cynical man, who had shown her so clearly what he thought of her and of her sex, was so directly opposed to all the dreams she had once held and cherished that it was as though that part of her emotions she had managed to blank off when Gerry hurt her had suddenly sprung into painful, hurting life; and, she thought miserably, how typical of her it was that the first time she should share such intimacy with a man had to be with one who had made it witheringly plain just how unappealing he found her.

What did she want, she asked herself crossly—to make love here in this cold, uncomfortable vehicle, with a man who was a stranger to her? Or was it simply that she wished for once in her life to see herself as desirable in a man's eyes? Did she simply ache for the panacea of knowing that, had she wanted to pursue it, the opportunity to arouse him sexually was there?

What was happening to her? she wondered nervously. Was it because she had spent the last four days witnessing the very obvious sexual chemistry between Gracie and Travis? Was it because she had known that at night the two of them were wrapped in one another's arms...sharing the kind of ecstasy she herself had once dreamed of knowing?

Horrible to see herself as the kind of person who could feel envious of another's happiness...who could actually bitterly resent the unfairness of a fate that had given her such yearning romantic ideals and, at the same time, ensured that her looks and her personality must make the fulfilment of those ideals nothing more than an impossible fantasy. Far better if she could have, as her mother had once said, settled for a dull, pragmatic husband and an equally dull, placid life, instead of yearning for the intensity of passion and desire.

She was quiet for so long that Matt actually began to think she was going to refuse. Idiotic woman, he fumed. Did she really think that he would actually want to take advantage of their intimacy, here in this uncomfortable and unromantic setting?

He shifted uncomfortably in his seat, wishing he had not had a sudden and disconcerting image of her lying on soft, clean sheets, her silky hair tumbling round her shoulders the way it had done while she was asleep, those amazing grey eyes slumberous with passion, that delicate, feminine body arched in eager supplication towards his own.

He ground his teeth, infuriated by his own weakness. It was that damned perfume she was wearing... it was conjuring up all manner of erotic images.

'Look, if you imagine that——'

'I'm not imagining anything,' Emily lied quickly, adding as calmly as she could, 'Of course, you're right. We have no option other than to share the sleeping-bag.' She gave a small shiver, aware that already she was getting cold and, worse, that her legs were slowly growing almost numb. It was that knowledge that provoked her into action.

'I'm afraid I'm going to have to take off my jeans,' she reminded him nervously.

'Yes,' he agreed tersely, wondering why on earth he was behaving like such a fool. Did he really prefer to risk suffering hypothermia than to matter-of-factly point out to her that both of them were likely to remain far warmer inside the sleeping-bag if they *both* removed their jeans and sweaters and allowed their combined body heat to circulate between them more effectively?

Emily's heart sank as he grimly announced these facts. She knew that he was speaking the truth, but the thought of lying next to him stripped down to her bra and briefs was a very daunting prospect.

'I think perhaps we should have a cup of coffee and a sandwich first,' she suggested hesitantly, waiting for him to mock her obvious reluctance to undress—but to her surprise he agreed, almost as though *he* felt as uncomfortable with the situation as she did herself.

It was a novel thought. Her only experience of male sexual behaviour was restricted to Gerry, and Gerry would have been very quick indeed to torment someone in her position. Gerry enjoyed inflicting emotional pain. She had quickly recognised that once the scales had been ripped from her eyes.

A little to her own astonishment she heard herself saying quietly, 'My father is in a local voluntary rescue team. I know he'd be the first to agree with everything you've said.'

His head came up and he looked at her. 'In that case I'm surprised he allowed you to drive anywhere tonight.'

Emily didn't tell him that her parents had themselves been on the verge of leaving, this time for the rain forests of Brazil. Instead of telling him this she said coolly, 'I'm an adult, not a child. I make my own decisions.'

She watched as his mouth compressed. He had a rather nice mouth beneath that straggly beard. His bottom lip was full and curved. She wondered hazily what it would feel like to touch it with her fingertips, and then swallowed nervously as her stomach plunged in shock at her own wayward thoughts.

'An adult! You're, what . . . eighteen? Nineteen?' He was scowling at her again.

'Actually,' she told him shakily, 'I'm twenty-six.'

Twenty-six! He stared at her. It must be because she was so small that she looked so much younger. Twenty-six . . . a woman, not a child . . . and so not innocent, either, despite the fact that those huge grey eyes seemed so unaware and unawakened.

'I'll get the coffee,' he told her austerely. 'You'd better get those jeans off.'

For such a large man he was surprisingly light on his feet, Emily reflected, as he managed to manoeuvre himself between the two front seats to crawl into the rear of the vehicle.

Her own hands had become awkward and clumsy, or perhaps it was the thick and unfamiliar fabric of the jeans that waywardly refused to respond to her demands. Whatever the cause, it seemed to take her ages to tug off the clammy fabric.

Once she had done so she was grateful for the huge oversized sweatshirt, which reached down almost to her knees . . . and not just for the warmth it offered, but because it concealed the minute briefness of her underwear which had been chosen because she had liked the pretty delicacy of the embroidered satin, and which she had never intended should be exposed to anyone's view other than her own. The cut of the briefs was such that they emphasised the feminine roundness of her hips and the length of her legs in a way which she was suddenly aware was very provocative indeed.

'Coffee?'

The curt voice from behind her made her swing round, causing Matt to wonder what on earth had put that look of sick misery in her eyes, unable to know that she had been thinking of Gerry, remembering how he had taunted her so cruelly, how he had found her so undesirable.

'You'd better get in the back,' Matt announced brusquely. 'It's getting dangerously cold in here. The sooner we're in that sleeping-bag, the happier I'll be.'

Acknowledging that he was right, Emily started to crawl awkwardly into the back of the Land Rover, totally unaware that, as she did so, the front of her sweatshirt was trapped beneath her body causing the back to ride up, so that Matt, automatically glancing into the driver's mirror, had a very clear and erotic view of the rounded curve of her bottom, more revealed than concealed by the brief scrap of satin clinging so seductively to her skin.

It infuriated him that he should continue to stare into the mirror for far longer than he would have wished, so that the way he finally took hold of her shoulders and virtually hauled her over the seat left Emily not only feeling bruised and breathless but also in no doubt of just how exasperating and irritating he found her presence.

She drank her coffee quickly, savouring its fragrant warmth, but decided that after all she didn't want to eat. Her stomach was churning nervously and she was having to fight hard not to look at the sleeping-bag Matt had unrolled, and to rigidly keep her back to him as she heard the small betraying sound that signified that he was removing his outer clothes.

She intended to keep on her sweatshirt until the last possible moment, all too conscious that her bra was every bit as revealing as her briefs, and so she waited until she was quite sure that all the slithering sounds which she suspected meant that Matt was climbing into the sleeping-bag had finished, before quickly tugging off her sweatshirt and hurriedly diving for the protective cover of the sleeping-bag.

Only Matt wasn't already in it. Instead, he was waiting grimly beside her. The sight of him—a shadowy, intimidatingly male figure with a bronze torso and a wedge of dark hair that arrowed downwards over a body that was less bulky and muscle-bound than she had envisaged to a pair of mercifully respectable boxer shorts—caught her unprepared. She froze and looked wildly for something to focus on other than his body, while he said frigidly, 'If you're quite ready, I think we'd both better get inside the sleeping-bag before either of us loses any more body heat.'

She was already shivering, her legs icy-cold from the knees downwards. Even so, she found herself hesitating, wishing there were some other way. But there wasn't, and she had no other option but to crawl into the sleeping-bag which he was holding open for her, to find that he had already put the car rug inside—which would account for the rustlings she had heard and which had deceived her into thinking he was already inside it.

There wasn't much space in the back of the Land Rover, and in order to get inside the sleeping-bag she had to wriggle past him. Her hip brushed against his arm, her skin quivering at the contact with the rough hairiness. Tiny flutters of sensation quivered to life deep in her stomach, an odd physical tension aching there. Shadowy insubstantial thoughts clouded her mind. Sometimes in her dreams she had felt like this, experienced this disturbing ache.

Shivering, she crawled into the sleeping-bag, keeping firmly to one side of it and lying with her back to its centre as she waited for him to join her. He was equally cautious—only there was a lot more of him than there was of her, and the sleeping-bag was not really designed for two people. It was inevitable that, as he slid down inside it, his body should brush hers, but what was surely not equally inevitable was the sensation that that brief contact should cause.

Once, she had desired Gerry, or she had thought she had, but even his most coaxing, skilful caresses had never aroused that sudden wanton spurt of awareness she had just experienced now. It must be her age, she told herself shakily as she lay rigid with shock. Either that or a reaction to Gracie's engagement... or perhaps her body was simply reacting physically to the intimacy she had sensed between Gracie and Travis.

It was ironic to remember that once she had daydreamed about just such an encounter, just such a stranger coming into her life and stirring her to immediate and reckless need and desire. Then it had seemed an idyllic romantic daydream; a thrilling fantasy of instant mutual awareness and responsiveness. Now that she was actually faced with the reality of experiencing urgent and extremely wanton physical yearning for a man who was a complete stranger, she was terrified by the implications of that desire, unable to understand why she was experiencing it.

It was just proximity, she told herself frantically... just a dangerous trick that her body was playing on her; but, as she felt the warmth of Matt's body reach out to engulf her, she held herself rigid with tension, genuinely appalled by the reactions of her own body, terrified of going to sleep in case in doing so she somehow or other betrayed what she was experiencing.

Matt didn't need his already low opinion of her sex reinforced by having to wake her up and point out to her that he did not find her sexually desirable. She could just imagine his reaction, were she in her sleep to give in to the lustful impulses that were filling her with such extraordinary and unfamiliar sensations.

She, who had never once in her life felt the slightest desire to make sexual advances to a man, and yet who was now unbelievably struggling not to give in to the mental temptation of allowing herself to imagine how it would feel to run her fingers over that dark wedge of body hair, to press her lips to that strong male throat... to...

'For God's sake, relax. I'm not going to touch you.'

The harsh command made her jump guiltily. No, *he* wasn't going to touch her, but *she*—she dared not make any response to him. It was safer to pretend that she was already asleep.

On his side of the sleeping-bag, Matt groaned and told himself that the discomfort in his body was caused by the fact that he hardly dared to breathe, never mind move. He could almost feel the tension emanating from the slim feminine body lying so close to his own.

What in hell's name did she think he was going to do? Did she really think he had so little control, so little respect for her as a fellow human being? But then, perhaps she had after all been aware of that far too lingering attention he had given the sight of her half-naked body. He closed his eyes and then opened them again as he was tormented by a mental image of his hands reaching out to close on the warm curves of her hips, to draw her back against his own body and turn her round and...

What the devil was the matter with him? Here he was, indulging in the most erotic kind of mental fantasies over a woman he knew absolutely nothing about, who probably already had a whole string of lovers, and who had made it more than plain that she had absolutely no desire to include him in their number.

No. Honesty compelled him to admit that his own extraordinary responsiveness to her had in no way been caused by any overt or covert sensual invitation on her part.

He only prayed that he did not turn over in his sleep and put his erotic fantasies into action. If he did, he had no doubt at all that his sleeping partner would be very caustic and acerbic in her denunciation of him—and quite rightly so.

Half an hour later, still wide awake and no closer to subduing his unruly body, Matt knew what he was going to have to do.

Emily felt him move beside her and tensed as she realised he was getting out of the sleeping-bag. 'What are you doing?' she asked him woodenly. Had she somehow or other communicated her feelings to him? She had been so careful not to touch him . . . not to allow her flesh to even brush against his, and yet humiliatingly it seemed he must be aware of what she was feeling.

'It just occurred to me that perhaps I ought to try and stay awake,' he lied. 'Someone might be trying to get through with the snow plough.'

Emily knew that he was lying. There was no way that they would attempt to clear the road until daylight. Outside the temperature was still dropping, and it was still snowing. She sat up, too emotionally disturbed for caution as she said shakily, 'You're lying. You know no one is going to attempt to clear this road tonight, and so do I.'

There was a small silence, and then he agreed almost curtly, 'All right, so I'm lying. If you must have the truth, dammit, you might as well have it— but I warn you, you won't like it. If I stay in here with you one more minute, I doubt that I'll be able to keep my hands off you.'

It was said so abruptly, so reluctantly, and with so much self-dislike that it was several seconds before what he was saying actually sank in. When it did, Emily felt her skin flush with brilliant colour, her voice as dazed as her brain as she whispered huskily, 'You can't mean that.'

'Perhaps I shouldn't mean it, but I'm afraid it's the truth. I want you in my arms, under my body— in the most intimate way it is possible for a man to want a woman,' he underlined almost savagely.

'And believe me, you can't be any more contemptuous of me than I am of myself. I assure you, I'm not——'

He broke off, leaving Emily to wonder what he had been about to say. He wasn't going to pretend he loved her...how could he? He wasn't going to apologise for wanting her? He wasn't going to actually put his physical desire into actions? Why not, when every sense she possessed was telling her how much she wanted that same intimacy with him which he had just described so brusquely. Wanted it...ached for it...yearned for it... She took one shaky breath and then another. This had to stop, and right now.

She opened her mouth to tell him so and instead, shockingly, incredibly, heard herself asking breathlessly, pleadingly almost, 'Do you really want to make love to me?' What was she saying? Where was she going? What was she doing, embarking down a road which could only go one way?

It seemed a long time before she heard his bleak, clipped, 'Yes...why?'

She took a deep breath, not allowing herself to think about what she was doing, holding fast to a deeper, more primitive instinct, like someone clutching a lifeline in heavy seas.

'I...I feel the same way.' When he was silent, she added, 'I want to make love with you.'

It was said...the need voiced. She had opened herself to him to accept—or reject—whichever he chose, and she could not begin to understand why she had done so. Only that she had responded to something within him that had struck an answering chord within her.

As she waited she said hesitantly, 'I can't pretend to understand why. I know I've probably shocked you. If you'd prefer not to...'

Opposite her, Matt tried to probe what lay behind the cool, well-mannered words—if she was simply playing a joke on him, trying to make a fool of him, or if she actually meant it. He tried to tell himself that there was no way he could feel this urgent, clamouring desire for a woman about whom he knew nothing at all other than that he wanted her, but his body refused to listen to such logic. His body was reinforcing what he already knew—his body...

Emily heard him mutter something under his breath and tensed, waiting for his rejection, her back held rigidly towards him.

And then, unbelievably, she felt his hands on her shoulders turning her towards him, his voice low and ragged as he said rawly, 'We shouldn't be doing this, you know...' He held her roughly as though pleading with her to deny him.

'No...I know...' Emily responded breathlessly, knowing even as she spoke that there was no power on earth that could stop this extraordinary mutual need that was driving them both.

And most extraordinary of all, she marvelled dizzily as she felt his arms close around her and draw her down against him, was the feeling she had of being so safe with him...so free to express herself and her desires, so free from restraint and shyness, so in tune with him that it was as though she had known him all her life, rather than a space of time that could be counted in minutes and hours instead of days and years

'If you should change your mind...' The words whispered against her lips, tantalising their soft flesh.

Here was her chance to hold back, to let caution and common sense hold sway, to withdraw from this madness which seemed to have possessed her—but ignoring it, rejecting the opportunity he was giving her, she heard herself saying almost fiercely, 'No...no. I don't want to change my mind...'

CHAPTER THREE

'YOU'RE sure you want this . . . Me?'

The words thrilled against her skin, raising a rash of gooseflesh, making her quiver and then tense as she felt Matt's lips tracing the shape of her mouth, exploring it, cherishing it so that her tension died in a flood of wonder and pleasure.

Why had she never known that it was possible to feel like this; that the delicate, almost hesitant touch of another mouth against her own could arouse her to such dizzying pleasure and need? It was as though this sensual exploratory meeting of their lips was something she had dreamed of— yearned for for an aeon of time, rather than knowing she wanted it only seconds before she experienced it.

Against Matt's mouth she whispered back, 'I want you,' and another thrill of anticipation ran through her as she felt the answering tension in Matt's body.

An unfamiliar heady eagerness to reach out to him and show him, with the touch of her hands and her lips, just what delight it gave her to have him near her overwhelmed her. She, who had never once initiated an embrace with any man—not even Gerry—had suddenly turned into a woman she could hardly recognise.

How had she known that the delicate touch of her fingertips against his skin would make Matt tense and groan against her mouth, tightening his hold on her, drawing her down against him so that her body was enveloped in the heat and maleness of his?

His hands cradled her head, his fingers sliding into her hair as his mouth explored the delicate contours of her face. His warm breath against her ear made her tremble and shiver beneath a shower of fiery darts of excitement. Sensations she had never known existed coiled through her stomach and swelled the soft curves of her breasts, inciting her to move with instinctive enticement against Matt's body, as her wanton flesh silently begged him to free it from the final barriers left between them.

She wanted to feel him against her, she recognised. She wanted to feel the hard heat of his skin against her own, to experience the touch of his hands and mouth against her body, and to explore the alien contours of his with hers. Her needs suspended reality and her ability to rationalise, her mind reeling under the shock of the dominating demands of her body.

As Matt's hand swept back her hair to lay bare her throat to the hungry assault of his mouth, she arched eagerly towards him, not in humble supplication, but in proud demand, knowing by some primitive instinct that, whatever the differences between them, in this their need for one another they met as equals.

The heat of his breath against her skin, the hard pressure of his mouth, the sharp bite of his teeth, the rough stroke of his hands on her skin, all of them were so perfectly attuned to her own needs that to experience them fed her desire at the same time as they momentarily satisfied it.

An instinct she hadn't known she possessed told her when to draw her own mouth against his flesh, when to stroke it tenderly with her tongue and when to graze it more ardently with the subtle pressure of her teeth.

Their surroundings, the storm which had brought them together, the fact that they were strangers to one another—all these had faded into insignificance. All that was important was that Matt had at last removed the last barriers of their underwear, and that his hands were cupping and shaping her breasts. That his thumbs were stroking eagerly, wonderingly almost, against the sensitive hardness of her nipples as though he knew exactly the intensity of her need to have him touch her just like that; as though he knew that even another second's delay in doing so would have stretched out the taut hot wire of desire that compelled her that little bit too far.

And, when he lowered his head and took one tender, flaunting nub of flesh into his mouth, caressing it gently with his lips and then his tongue, raking it less gently with his teeth and then finally sucking so erotically and rhythmically on it that her whole body turned fluid and pulsed in a shockingly arousing harmony with it, it was as though she had waited for this moment, this pleasure . . . this man, for an infinity of time.

What she was experiencing went far beyond right or wrong, far, far beyond worrying about doing the right thing...about defending herself from hurt and pain. This need they were sharing was so elemental, so fierce, so overpowering that it cut across every layer of civilisation, laying bare the deepest essences of their humanity.

The Emily she had always known, had always been, would rather have died a thousand deaths than cry out in a pleasure that was almost pain at the sheer impossibility of containing what she was feeling—what he was making her feel. The Emily she had thought of herself as being could never have imagined herself wanting to share with any man her joy in the pleasure he was giving her—wanting to tell him, to show him, to give to him in equal measure all that he was so generously giving to her. The Emily she had thought she was would never have eagerly and openly murmured her need when Matt turned his head to caress her other breast as he had done its twin.

'Francine... I can't believe this is happening. You're...'

Emily tensed. Francine. She had forgotten about that. Would he have wanted her the same if she had told him she was Emily? A rose by any other name...

Francine. Perhaps it was being Francine that gave her the freedom to behave in a way that Emily could never have behaved.

Matt's mouth touched her stomach, sending tiny pulses of electric sensation coiling through her, making tiny nerve-endings beneath her skin beat frantically in excitement. His hand stroked her hip; soon...

'No. Not yet,' she told him huskily. 'I want to...' She stopped, realising that she had almost said 'I want to love you.' What words did you use to tell

a man that you wanted to explore and enjoy the
sensation of his flesh beneath your hands and
mouth the way he had done yours? That you wanted
to give him the same pleasure he had given you;
that you wanted to share with him your joy in the
fact that he *was* a man?

If they existed she had no idea what they were,
and so, while he hesitated, she simply asked softly,
'Can I do this?' and then placed her mouth against
his body, tentatively tracing the aureole of his
nipple, so different from hers—and yet, perhaps in
some ways not so very different after all, she decided as she felt him shudder and move restlessly
against her, his hands gripping her waist and then
stroking up over her body before he buried them
in her hair, silently urging her to repeat the caress,
and then not so silently as she fulfilled his silent
command and experienced the satisfaction of
feeling his body shudder in immediate response to
her touch.

Why had she never guessed there would be a time,
a man, with whom all the barriers of protection
and self-preservation would simply be swept away;
a man whose body aroused her to such heights of
both tenderness and desire that the sound of
helpless need he made in his throat when her mouth
touched the taut plane of his belly almost made her
eyes sting with tears. He was so vulnerable to her—
as vulnerable as she was to him. With Gerry, sexual
intimacy had been something she had always
secretly feared. She had analysed that fear as a fear
of her own lack of experience, of disappointing
him, of being found inadequate; but now, with
Matt, there was no fear, no hesitation, nothing that

could mar the fierce surge of joy that touching him brought her. Where she had only felt fierce feminine pride in her own responsiveness to his touch, now that she was the one to arouse him, to strip him of all the veneer of civilisation and lay bare his essential maleness, she did feel humbled, softened, awed by the strength of his response to her.

His hands rested fleetingly on her shoulders as though he meant to urge her away from him, and then, when her tongue deliberately followed the soft line of hair that ran down from his navel, he tensed and writhed, torn between protest and need, moaning a contradictory burst of staccato pleas.

She ignored everything he was saying. This was her pleasure as well as his; her need, her desire. They would only have this one night, and now, while her soul and her body were so receptive to him that it was almost as though he was actually a part of her, she wanted to share with him all her joy, to pour out over him the gift of her body's desire for him.

Beneath her hands and mouth, Matt cried out her name. Once, long ago, he had wanted to love Jolie like this and be loved by her in turn, but she had hated it when he had touched her breasts and kissed them. He had blamed himself for his inability to arouse her; had blamed his own lack of skill and sensitivity. Women could and did enjoy sex, as he had discovered during his teenage years, but although Jolie had been quite willing to allow him the intimacy of her body he had known that there was no reciprocal joy in it for her.

He had told himself that he must exercise restraint, that his love for her would show him the way to give her pleasure, that he must control his own desires and think first of her. And then he had found her in bed with someone else.

One of his friends at the time had told him that he was better off without her, describing her as a cold bitch who liked to tease. How would that same friend have described the woman in his arms now, he wondered hazily, his mind dissolving in the heat that lapped his body.

There was nothing calculated or self-seeking about the way she was touching him . . . loving him. She had no artifice . . . no tricks. She aroused him in a way he had never experienced before; she made him feel more like a god than a man, he acknowledged shakily as his senses rioted beneath the delicate exploration of her mouth against his flesh. Her mouth . . . He shuddered violently beneath its caress, hearing the soft purring sound of pleasure she made in her throat, before he caught hold of her and said roughly, 'No. It's been too long,' and then, in a lower, rawer voice that locked the muscles in her throat, Emily heard him whisper huskily in her ear, 'When it happens, I want to be inside you; if you keep on touching me like that . . .'

Her stomach seemed to somersault inside her as he drew her down against him and she felt the hard, male weight of him resting between her thighs. Her body was open, moist, eager to feel his flesh within it.

He hesitated, and for a moment fear touched her. Then he said quietly, 'It's not too late . . . to change your mind.'

Emily didn't speak. She couldn't. Instead, she slid her hands down over him in deliberate invitation, arching up to meet him as he moved against her and then within her.

It was like nothing she had ever imagined: an indescribable maelstrom of sensations, a sudden sharp dart of surprise that, despite her readiness, her eagerness for this moment, she should still experience the age-old thrill of feminine fear at this first possession by a maleness that was suddenly so much more male and overpowering than she had realised.

But even as the fear struck Matt was kissing her, causing her body to flood with such heat that the fear melted, and the brief, unexpected spasm of discomfort was gone before she had time to react to it, leaving her body free to respond to the rhythm Matt's was teaching it. The rhythm of life itself, Emily recognised hazily as her senses opened out in response to all that she was feeling in the same way that her body opened itself to the pleasure of experiencing Matt's possession of it, so that a sharp escalating urgency soon overtook her feminine triumph at her body's ability to hold and arouse him. Beyond that urgency lay something she just had to reach, somewhere she just had to be, all her senses striving eagerly towards it, so that when she did finally reach it she cried out without knowing she did so, and then cried out again as she felt the hot pulse of Matt's release inside her.

As she lay supine and exhausted in his arms, she thought dizzily that there was something she ought to say... something she ought to do, but her body was now as greedy for sleep as it had been for completion. It felt so right lying here next to Matt—so very right...

As she drifted into sleep, Matt stared into the darkness. He was not a promiscuous man. There had been women, of course, but his experience with Jolie had taught him that sex alone was not sufficient. And as for love... He wasn't sure he believed any longer that sexual love could exist.

He had no idea why this had happened tonight... Why he had felt this intense desire—this compulsive need for this woman who was a stranger to him, and yet, at the same time, so familiar to him that he might have known her always.

She had given herself to him freely and joyfully. She muttered something in her sleep, curling towards him. He leaned down, and brushed the hair away from her face. In the morning there would be faint bruises on her skin where he had loved her, while he... He flexed his back and grimaced. He was on his way to start a new life, to take up a new post. The last thing he needed right now was any kind of emotional complication. And the last thing he could do after tonight was to ignore what had happened and to pretend that the woman sleeping in his arms did not exist. Not now. Not ever.

It was the sound of male voices which eventually woke Emily. She came to reluctantly and groggily, conscious of several things at once, none of them particularly pleasant: she was cold and her body ached, from sleeping on the hard floor of the Land Rover her spine felt as though someone had walked up and down it, and there was another ache as well, less easy to define—and then abruptly she remembered, her fingers automatically gripping the protection of the sleeping-bag more tightly around her as the full details of the previous night came flooding back.

What on earth had she done...and why...? In the cold light of day, the overwhelming force of the need which had driven her seemed impossible to accept or explain. She was alone in the Land Rover; she could hear Matt talking to someone outside, which must mean that the road was clear.

Someone, not herself she was sure, had folded her clothes and placed them easily within her reach. There was no one to see the hot tide of colour that burned her skin as she reached for them, hurriedly dressing beneath the protective cover of the sleeping-bag.

What on earth was she going to have to say to Matt? How was she going to face him? A memory from the previous night washed slowly through her: an echo of passion...of closeness, of giving, of love—but no, that was impossible. Theirs had simply been a brief coming together of two people whose momentary need had overwhelmed their common sense.

Now, with that desire deadened, Emily suffered a sickening sensation of shocked bewilderment that she could ever have behaved the way she had, a sense of self-revulsion she could not quell.

She heard Matt rap briefly on the side of the Land Rover, as though in warning, before he opened the door. In the harsh, snowlit light of day, his unruly hair and untidy growth of beard looked even more raffish than they had done the night before. But then, she supposed she looked little better, Emily thought tiredly, conscious of her crumpled sweatshirt and creased, although dry, jeans.

'That was the snow plough,' Matt told her unnecessarily. 'I've warned him about your car. Now that the road's cleared we might as well be on our way. Is there anywhere special you want me to drop you?'

Yes, the largest, deepest hole he could find, Emily thought miserably, all too conscious of the way, after one brief, uncertain glance in her direction, he had avoided looking at her.

It was all right for him, she told herself bitterly. He was a man, no doubt accustomed to these casual, meaningless encounters. Silently lashing herself with twin whips of guilt and self-contempt, she kept her back to him as she asked if he would drop her in the small market town on the other side of the hills. From there she could ring Uncle John and find a garage to rescue her car.

'There's some coffee left,' she heard Matt saying hesitantly behind her. 'If you ...'

She couldn't speak. For some reason, there was an enormous lump in her throat. Last night, in his arms, she had felt as though they were two halves of a perfect whole. This morning ... this morning she couldn't understand the fever which had driven her into those arms in the first place; and then, illuminatingly, as she turned round abruptly and looked at him, something inside her seemed to turn over and melt.

As he watched her, Matt wished he knew what to say; last night she had been so warm, so eager ... This morning she was so cold and withdrawn, making it very plain that last night was now a forgotten incident. The trouble was that it had been so long since he had been involved with a woman that he had come close to forgetting the rules. He'd heard enough ... read enough about this new breed of woman who felt uninhibited enough and free enough to take her sexual pleasure where she chose without making any kind of emotional commitment to her partner, but this was the first time he had experienced this new feminine sexual freedom. He wanted to reach out and touch her, to tell her how much last night had meant to him, but her whole manner indicated how much she now wanted to distance herself from him. He cursed himself for his weakness in wanting to establish some sort of emotional bonding with her.

Traditionally it was women who wanted and needed more from a man than the physical pleasure of his body. Hadn't he already learned his lesson with Jolie? Hadn't he learned then that not all women desired or needed love?

He climbed into the front seat of the Land Rover, relieved when the engine turned over first time. The atmosphere inside the vehicle was strained and tense, almost as though they were two enemies forced together, and yet last night ...

Forget last night, he told himself harshly. She...Francine...an exotic name and yet one that jarred him somehow. She looked so soft and fragile sitting there in that huge sweatshirt, her face virtually free of make-up, her hair a silky veil that concealed her expression. Last night he had threaded that silky softness through his fingers, and felt its warmth against his skin. Last night she had made no secret of the pleasure she had found in his arms. This morning she was as cold and remote as the snow-covered hills outside.

What was the matter with him, he derided himself, that he felt this need to look for something more than a mere casual sexual encounter; why did he have this feeling of loss, of betrayal, almost? Why did he persist in feeling as though last night had been something special and precious, a gift for him alone?

There had been nothing shy or hesitant about the way she had touched him, nothing uninformed or uncertain in the caresses that had burned his skin and made him ache so much. And yet... He clamped down hard on his wayward thoughts. It had happened and now it was over, she had made that clear enough...

As she sat miserable and silent beside him, Emily wondered what on earth Matt must be thinking of her. The very fact that he hadn't referred to last night proved how little it must have meant to him. If he had just said something, made a gesture towards her... but why should he? He had given her the opportunity to draw back last night. She hadn't taken it, so how could she blame him now for assuming that such casual and meaningless sexual encounters were a normal part of her life? After all, she had hardly behaved like a shy, inexperienced virgin, had she?

Her face burned as she remembered exactly how she had behaved; even now it astounded her that she had had that primitive, intimate knowledge of how to please and arouse him. Never once had she been tempted to caress Gerry the way she had wanted—no, needed—to caress Matt . . . never once with Gerry had she experienced that delirious awareness of her own female power.

The silence of the snow-bound countryside was all around them. They were over the top now and dropping down towards the small town where Matt would leave her. They would never meet again. That was what she wanted, wasn't it, so why did she have this ridiculous desire to burst into tears?

They had reached the outskirts of the town. Soon they would be going their separate ways. When she had first woken up this morning, and realised what she had done, she had felt that she would die if she ever had to see Matt again, and now, when they were about to part, deep inside her she felt a tearing, wrenching sense of acute pain, as though the last thing she wanted was to leave him ever again.

'I'll drop you in the centre of the town, shall I?' Matt asked her roughly.

Emily nodded her head; her throat was too raw with pain for her to speak. The roughness in Matt's voice, which disguised his reluctance to let her go, she interpreted as impatience to get rid of her, and when he stopped the Land Rover at a convenient place she had the door open and was halfway out before he could do anything to stop her. If she hadn't had to wait for him to hand her her things, he suspected that she'd have disappeared out of his sight without even saying goodbye.

As she took her bag from him and their fingers touched, an electric charge burned his flesh, reminding him of last night's passion. He wanted to say something to her, to reassure her that if there should be any repercussions... but a woman who made love so eagerly and so skilfully would never take those kind of risks. Which was just as well, because he certainly hadn't given any thought in the heat of their lovemaking to the possibility that she might conceive his child. He wanted to reach out to her, to hold on to her, but he knew that if he tried she would rebuff him. He had her name— the make of her car. He could always trace her...

And yet still he was tempted to hold on to her, to make her stay with him, to tell her how much last night had meant to him, how unexpected it had been, that need for her—the feeling of oneness, of rightness, of needing...of loving?

As she walked away from him, Emily wondered if her legs would actually support her. She felt so weak, so shaky, so vulnerable and alone in a way she had never experienced before. That brief meeting of their fingers had run through her like lightning.

Forget him, she instructed herself as she refused to give in to the temptation to look back at him. Forget him and forget last night. It's over...finished. You'll never see him again and you ought to be glad of it.

CHAPTER FOUR

'EMILY, I'll be bringing a colleague home with me tonight. In fact, he'll probably be staying here for a while until he finds his feet, so to speak. He's an ex-pupil of mine who's taking over the Modern History Chair from Peregrine Myers for a trial period of six months. I meant to mention it to you earlier. He rang me while you were staying with your parents.'

Emily sighed. It wasn't unusual for her great-uncle to bring a colleague home with him; occasionally they stayed overnight, but there was certainly enough room in the rambling old house to accommodate half a dozen visitors if necessary. However, Emily was remembering that it was almost a month since she had last been to the supermarket and stocked up, and, for all their often fragile appearances, her great-uncle's colleagues always seemed to have hearty appetites. There would be a room to prepare as well, and she had just got to a particularly complicated part of Uncle John's notes.

'You've got that man from the publishers coming to see you tomorrow,' she warned him. 'Now you will remember, won't you?'

Her uncle had a notoriously bad memory and she was not altogether surprised that he had forgotten to mention the arrival of his colleague.

Down here in the south, it already felt like spring. The snowdrops were gone and the daffodils were nodding their golden heads in the gardens and under the hedges.

It was a month since she had visited her parents. A month since... her hands started to shake and she forced herself to banish the memories crowding her mind. Since her return from the borders there hadn't been a single night when she hadn't been tormented by dreams... by memories, and then more recently by fears, which thankfully had been banished earlier this week when her body had given her irrefutable proof that her idiotic and senseless behaviour had not created a child.

For that she was profoundly grateful, and yet at the same time there had been a sharply poignant sense of loss in the knowledge that physically she would have nothing to remind her of that shared night with Matt.

Not that she had wanted to conceive. She wasn't equipped to bring up a child alone; she didn't have the strength, the inner resources, and yet—and yet to have loved a man so intensely, to have been loved by him so intensely in turn that that loving had created a new life...

She told herself that her feelings were sheer emotionalism; that men who raped could impregnate their victims; that many, many children were conceived in an act that had nothing of love in it, and yet that vague feeling of loss had persisted until she had grown impatient both with it and with herself.

She had behaved like an idiot and the best thing she could do was to put the whole thing out of her mind and be grateful that she was free to do so. She still had no idea what on earth had compelled her to behave the way she had; but the initial shock and searing shame which had so stunned her had gone, leaving an odd guilty awareness that it was the pleasure of those hours she remembered most, and not the sick feeling of self-disgust which had followed them.

To have made love, so passionately, so intensely with a stranger—it was so out of character for her. Half of her still did not truly believe she had done it; perhaps she hadn't, she reflected fancifully half an hour later, driving into town—perhaps she had just imagined the whole thing. If so, her imagination was far more powerful than she had ever realised.

She parked and did her shopping with her customary efficiency. While she had been at home, Gracie had complained exasperatedly that Emily was allowing Uncle John to turn her into more of a housekeeper-cum-companion than the highly qualified research assistant she was trained to be.

'With your qualifications, your intelligence, you could work anywhere,' Gracie had expostulated when Emily had said placidly that she enjoyed the variety of her life with their great-uncle. And it was true—she did. Despite his absent-mindedness, her great-uncle had a brilliant brain, and Emily had discovered during the time she had been working for him that she was becoming as fascinated by the ancient Egyptians as he was himself.

She hoped that the publishers would have some good news for him at their meeting. The publication of his book meant a great deal to him.

As she stowed her shopping away in her car, she glanced at her watch and reflected that, with a bit of luck, she should just make it back to the house in time to warn Mrs Beattie about their unexpected visitor.

When Emily had first come to work for her uncle, it had taken a great deal of tact and diplomacy to establish good relations with the woman who had been coming in to clean for her uncle two days a week for almost twenty years, but, once she had realised that Emily was not going to trespass on her territory, the two of them had established a good working relationship.

This summer, with a bit of luck, she really might be able to persuade Uncle John to do something about restoring his half-wild garden to something approaching order, she decided as she drove home.

In addition to its overgrown flower beds and wilderness of a lawn, the house also had a walled kitchen garden. It seemed a shocking waste to Emily that they weren't taking advantage of this benefit and producing their own vegetables. With a bit of luck, if she could persuade Uncle John to get someone in to tidy the garden up a bit, she might be able to find the time to grow the vegetables herself.

She knew that her parents and sister found it hard to understand this craving she had for settled roots, for permanency. What her mother termed her 'domesticity' was something alien to the rest of the family, all of whom seemed to have been either a restless adventuring type like her parents and sister, or great academics like her uncle.

The notion that someone might actually find pleasure in running a home, in cooking and gardening, in providing the material comforts for others, was so foreign to her family's way of life that Emily had for a long time striven to deny the need within herself to do these things. Now that she was older she had learned to accept this side of her nature and to channel it as productively as she could.

What she really needed, Gracie had told her forthrightly, was a home of her own and a large family to go with it. 'If you must be so horribly domestic, darling, then at least find yourself a gorgeous mate to provide you with a brood of kids. It seems such a waste thinking of you lavishing all that time and attention on someone like Uncle John. Let's face it, he's so wrapped up in his mummies, he hardly notices anything else.'

Emily had shrugged her shoulders and pretended that her sister's comment hadn't hurt. Gracie hadn't meant to hurt her—she knew that. It would simply never occur to her that a woman might yearn desperately for what she had so casually termed a mate and a brood of kids, and yet know at the same time that those longings were unlikely to be fulfilled. At least, not in the idealistic manner of Emily's private daydreams.

The world was changing and there no longer seemed to be a place in it for a woman like her. These days women were expected to want careers, to be ambitious, to juggle the demands of work, husbands and families, and still have time left over to look glamorous and worldly.

Having it all, it was called. Emily grimaced to herself. Did no one realise yet that it was virtually impossible for any one human being, no matter how highly motivated, to reach such relentless standards of perfection, and that there were many, many women who, when faced with the impossibility of matching such a role model, felt that such unattainable heights of perfection only underlined their own inadequacies? Women were good at feeling guilty, Emily acknowledged; and now they were being given additional burdens of guilt to carry.

Frowning a little over her introspective mood, which she knew full well was caused by her unwanted memories of Matt, she forced herself to concentrate on her driving instead of giving in to the self-indulgence of useless daydreams.

Face it, she told herself cruelly, what happened meant nothing to him; it was just a brief sexual fling. You could have been anyone. Telling herself that helped to underline her self-contempt. What kind of woman was she? she asked herself bitterly as she stopped the car and started to unload the shopping, carrying it into the big old-fashioned kitchen, and putting the boxes on the scrubbed deal table. Was she really so insecure, so desperate that she had had to give herself sexually to the first man who had asked her—the only man who had asked her? she reminded herself mercilessly. Was she really so incomplete in herself that she had needed a stranger's touch on her body to reinforce her sexuality?

Her emotions protested that it hadn't been like that, but the sterner, more critical side of her nature derided this weakness. It was useless trying to hide from the truth. The only good thing about the whole affair was that she was not pregnant, and that she would never have to face Matt again.

She could hear Mrs Beattie moving about upstairs, and, telling herself that there had been enough emotional self-indulgence for one day, she went upstairs to warn her about the arrival of Uncle John's colleague.

Mrs Beattie was thorough but slow, and by the time, with Emily's help, the most habitable of the spare bedrooms had been prepared for Uncle John's colleague, there was barely time for Emily to check through the post to make sure that nothing urgent needed to be dealt with before starting on the preparation of the evening meal.

Uncle John preferred plain food cooked and served in a traditional manner, although Emily occasionally mourned the fact that this prevented her from giving her more artistic culinary talents their head.

This evening she had planned on serving a warming beef stew with dumplings, which she knew was one of his favourites. She only hoped that his colleague shared her great-uncle's fondness for what Emily privately thought of as rather dull boarding-school fare. After dinner she would leave the two old men together while she got on with some more work on her uncle's notes.

Her uncle wrote out his notes in a cramped, almost indecipherable hand which initially she had found it almost impossible to read, but now, with the ease of long practice, she skimmed through the handwritten sheets beside her typewriter, and then settled down to read them more thoroughly.

It had been an additional bonus that the long summer vacations of her university days had prompted her to take a short, intensive secretarial course, primarily in those days so that she could earn extra money to pad out her grant; but, since coming to work for her great-uncle, she had found her secretarial skills almost as important as her abilities as a researcher.

As always, once she started to transcribe her uncle's notes she quickly found herself so deeply embroiled in the characters unfolding in front of her that they became more real to her than her surroundings.

Guiltily she acknowledged that she was probably culpable of humanising the bare bones of her uncle's research to such an extent that his learned treatise on the everyday life of a wealthy merchant and his family and their position within the complex social hierarchy of Egypt was beginning to read more like a novel than a set of interlinking facts.

However, whenever she passed over the completed pages for her uncle to read, he seemed quite happy with what she had produced; and, if certain small humanising details came from the odd snippets of information she herself had picked up when checking up for her uncle on certain previous research he had done, Uncle John himself seemed unaware of it.

She was so engrossed in what she was doing that the striking of the grandfather clock in the hall outside the study, reminding her that it was five o'clock and that her uncle and his friend would soon be coming in, made her sigh in mild frustration and put her work to one side.

Although the house was centrally heated, her uncle always insisted on having an open fire burning in whichever room he was using, and Emily's first task, after she had covered her typewriter and put away her work, was to go into the dining-room and put a match to the fire she had set in there earlier.

The dining-room was a dark-panelled area which she was constantly trying to enliven and warm with the addition of bowls and jugs of flowers. Today a large pewter jug of daffodils and forsythia from the garden cast a warm pool of golden sunshine over the polished darkness of the oak sideboard.

While she kept one eye on the fire to make sure that it wasn't going to go out—it had appalled her to discover when she first came to live with and work for her uncle that none of the chimneys had been swept in over five years, and the dining-room chimney especially had a habit of belching smoke sulkily when the wind was in the wrong direction—she started to prepare the polished oak refectory table for dinner.

Her uncle, like most males of his generation, enjoyed a little cosseting, and Emily was quite happy to indulge him in this small vice. She knew how much he liked sitting down to dinner at a table set with the heavy polished cutlery he had inherited from his Victorian grandparents, and the equally old and treasured Meissen dinner service.

When she had finished she surveyed the room, with its warm, burning fire, its polished wood, its gleaming silver and its red and gold-banded china, and she wondered if her great-uncle had the faintest idea of just how much work went into the production of such a welcoming setting, and how much more work there would be after dinner was over.

Each piece of the precious, fragile china had to be carefully washed and dried by hand, each piece of cutlery polished—tasks which Emily always felt it was unfair to leave to Mrs Beattie.

And yet at heart she didn't really mind. There was something very satisfying about knowing she was, if only indirectly, responsible for such a welcoming scene. Another instance of how unfitted she was for modern life, she decided as she headed back to the kitchen. She could certainly never envisage herself in a role where she called any human being her superior, but this need she had to find an outlet for her homemaking instincts seemed to get stronger rather than weaker as time passed.

Her uncle would expect to sit down to dinner at half-past eight; he would want to give his guest a glass of the expensive dry sherry he favoured first, and of course the man would have to be shown his room and given time to settle in. Emily sighed as she glanced at her watch. Half-past six. She hoped her uncle wasn't going to be too much longer.

Almost on cue she heard a car arriving outside, its soft, subtle purr surely indicating a machine far more expensive than the diesel-fuelled vehicles belonging to the taxi firm her uncle always used when she wasn't driving him. She frowned as she took off her apron, automatically smoothing the plain, neat front of her dark grey dress before stepping into the hall.

The door opened. She heard her uncle's voice, and then another: male, vibrant, and shockingly familiar. She stood frozen where she was, while the effect of that voice was like an electric shock to her system. Disbelief, fear, anger, shock; all of them flowed through her in a jangling discordant series of silently screamed protests.

Matt! But it couldn't be. Not here!

Her head was swimming; she felt sick and dizzy, her heart beating rapidly so that she almost felt as though she were hyperventilating. She forced herself to take a deep, calming breath and then another as she stood in a betrayingly defensive position, her back almost up against the panelling of the hallway as she instinctively sought protection in the shadows.

Her uncle walked in first, his conversation and walk more animated than Emily remembered it being for a long time, and then Matt followed him—but a different Matt from the one she remembered.

Gone was the ragged hair and beard, and in its place was a smoothly shaved and intensely masculine jaw. The untidy, overlong hair had been cut, the jeans and sweater replaced by the standard don's uniform of sports jacket .well worn at the elbows, beneath which he was wearing a checked shirt and a plain tie. It was odd how her brain retained the facility to monitor and record these small, so unimportant details, while her body refused to free itself from the sick tension that chained her to where she stood.

'I'll just introduce you to my niece. Marvellous girl. I wonder...'

She saw her uncle peering myopically around him, and forced herself to move.

The silent prayer she was uttering that by some miracle Matt wouldn't recognise her went unanswered as she stepped shakily out of the shadows, and monitored with acute anxiety the immediate recognition that widened his eyes and then narrowed them as he focused on her with an intensity that made her stomach churn.

'Ah, Emily, my dear, there you are. Come and let me introduce you to our guest. Matt... this is my niece, or rather, my great-niece, and assistant, Emily Blacklaw. Emily, this is the colleague I was telling you about—Matt.'

Far faster to recover than she could ever have been, Matt was extending his hand towards her. She put her own into it reluctantly, all too conscious of the hardness of the calluses on his palms, calluses which had brushed her skin and sensitised it to heights of almost unbearable desire.

'Emily...'

That faint hardening of tone as he said her name wasn't something she had imagined, she knew, and, despite all the efforts of her self-control, she could do nothing to prevent the hot, guilty tide of colour staining her skin. She couldn't speak, and she knew that the effort she made to smile and behave normally fell a long, long way short of his own almost urbane reaction to her.

But then, he had probably had a lot more practice at this sort of thing than she had had herself, she reflected bitterly, remembering how, when he had touched her, there had been nothing tentative or unknowing about the movement of his hands and mouth.

Sublimely unconscious of the ferocity of the hidden currents surging between his niece and his colleague, her uncle said, good-humouredly, 'Emily, perhaps you'd show Matt his room, and then, if you'd like to join me in my study for a pre-dinner glass of sherry, Matt . . .'

There was nothing she could do—no escape route she could take. Rigidly keeping her back to him, Emily walked towards the stairs. She knew he was following her, even though he moved so lightly that she couldn't hear his footsteps.

She waited tensely for her uncle to open his study door, her fingers tightening on the banister rail as she felt the heat of Matt's body close behind her on the stairs. Every instinct she possessed urged her to forget pride and everything else, and to take to her heels and run, but before she could do any such thing she felt his fingers closing round her wrist, forcing her to stand still as he caught up with her.

Some last spark of bravado made her say haughtily, 'Yes . . . what is it?'

The look he gave her was glacial. 'I'm surprised you need to ask. I'm introduced to the great-niece of a colleague, a young woman by the name of Emily Blacklaw, but I already know that same young woman by a completely different name. I think in the circumstances some explanation is merited, don't you?'

'Francine is my second name,' Emily told him stiffly.

'And a convenient disguise to hide behind, should I have tried to follow up our . . . er, acquaintance.'

Emily compressed her lips. They both knew that there was scant chance that he would have wanted to do that, but it was impossible to tell him why she had lied. Why just for once she had wanted to be someone other than herself.

'You must think what you wish,' she told him curtly. 'I don't have to explain myself to you.'

'No, indeed,' he agreed. He was watching her almost gravely, an expression in his eyes that made her body feel as though it were covered in scalding heat. This confrontation with him, so unexpected and so unwanted, was bringing home to her, if she needed it reinforcing, the full intensity of the sordidness of their encounter.

Inwardly writhing with self-disgust, forcing herself to forget that in his arms she had felt neither guilt nor any loss of self-respect, but rather the reverse—that she had in fact felt loved, cherished, desired, wanted, loved...

'But you didn't want me to find you, did you?'

Alarm bells were starting to ring in her brain. Why did he keep asking her that? Surely he had as little desire to meet her again as she had him?

'I can't think of any reason why either of us should want to see the other again,' she told him stiffly.

'Can't you?' The look in his eyes made her stomach twist sharply. Heat suddenly flooded her, a heat which had nothing at all to do with the searing, burning self-disgust she had felt earlier. A heat that had its roots in the dangerous wanton ache that was so quickly and treacherously infiltrating her body. She could think of only one reason why he might have wanted to see her again. She shuddered as she stood staring defiantly into his eyes. Did he really think that she would be willing to indulge in a sordid sexual liaison with him—a liaison through which they both indulged their sexual needs without any softening, lifting, shared emotional commitment? What sort of woman did he think she was? She bit her lip in mortification, suddenly unable to look at him any longer. It was obvious just what he thought she was, and with good reason.

'Of course,' he was saying coolly, 'there could be another reason why you deliberately concealed your real identity. It could be that there is already someone else in your life. Someone for whom I was used as a substitute...' His voice hardened dangerously over the last word, but, oblivious to her danger, Emily reached eagerly for the lifeline he had unwittingly thrown her.

Someone else... Yes, that was it. She would have to pretend that there *was* someone else, for the duration of his visit at least. That way she could ensure that he didn't make any attempt to repeat the intimacies they had shared so unexpectedly and so dangerously.

Quite how she knew that he was a man who would never accept being used in the way he had just described to her, she had no idea, but that knowledge was like a life-raft and she clung desperately to it, heedless of the reckless note of desperation in her own voice as she said quickly, 'Yes. Yes, there is someone else——'

She broke off as the study door opened and her uncle came out. 'Emily,' he called up to her, seeing her standing on the stairs. 'There's a telephone call for you. Someone called Travis.'

'Travis.'

What on earth was her sister's fiancé ringing her for? Had there been an accident? Was something wrong with Gracie?

As she started to hurry downstairs, tugging her wrist free of Matt's confining grip, he leaned forward and said menacingly, 'Travis—and just who is he?'

Later she had no idea what on earth had made her say it; it was so out of character for her to lie— and such a mammoth and idiotic lie as well, but then, everything she had done when she was in Matt Slater's company was out of character, so that her quick, automatic lie of, 'Travis is my fiancé,' tripped off her tongue so easily and so unexpectedly that she could hardly believe she had actually spoken the words.

As she hurried into the study, she found that her heart was beating at what seemed to be twice its normal rate. She picked up the receiver with a hand that shook visibly; curling her fingers round it, she said tensely, 'Travis, it's Emily. Is anything wrong?'

'No...no, nothing like that. It's just that my folks are planning a trip to England. They're leaving in three months' time, they both want to visit your part of the world and Gracie suggested that your uncle might be able to put them up for a couple of days and that you might be able to show them around. Feel free to say no, if it's going to be too much trouble.'

Trouble... She wanted to laugh in sheer hysteria. Trouble was the man she had left standing on the stairs. Trouble was the feeling she got inside when she looked at him. Trouble was the sick, awful knowledge that she had got herself into a situation completely beyond her experience—a situation she had no hope of being able to cope with.

'No,' she heard herself saying. 'It won't be any trouble. If you could just let me have the dates when your parents will be here...'

They chatted for a few more minutes; her sister, it seemed, was out shopping with her mother-in-law-to-be, and, conscious both of the cost of the call and the fact that Matt Slater was probably still standing on the stairs waiting for her, Emily said her goodbyes as quickly as she could.

He was, and he broke off his conversation with her great-uncle when she reappeared, waiting until they were out of earshot to demand abruptly, 'Why didn't you *tell* me you were engaged?'

'You never asked.'

There was an unexpectedly grim silence, almost as though he was angry with her, but why should he be?

'I see. Where is he? Why isn't he with you?'

'He had to go back to Australia.'

'And because *he* wasn't available, you made love with me, as a substitute—is that it?' he accused.

They were outside his room now. Emily stopped, wishing she could find a way of ending this awful ordeal. Keeping her face averted, she shrugged nonchalantly and, she felt, unconvincingly.

'I...I suppose I was missing him so much that...' Her voice trailed off uncomfortably as she tried and failed to imagine herself, if she had been engaged to anyone, actually making love with someone else.

'You were missing him so much that you used me to relieve your sexual need.' He sounded furiously, bitterly angry, Emily recognised numbly, and hearing it put into words, and such words, made her shudder with self-loathing—but there was no way out now.

'Yes. Yes, I'm afraid I did.'

There was an odd quality to his silence, but she couldn't risk looking at him to see why. 'This is your room,' she told him stiffly, pushing open the door. 'I'll leave you to settle in. Uncle John likes to have dinner at eight-thirty.'

She was starting to turn away from him when he reached out and took hold of her arm, restraining her. 'Tell me something,' he enquired softly. 'Is there any likelihood that you're—er...going to miss this fiancé of yours while I'm staying here as a guest of your uncle? Because if there is...'

This was what she had been dreading. What she had tried to protect herself against, ever since she had stood in the hallway and seen that sharp, assessing look in his eyes.

It was worse, far worse than anything she could have imagined. The humiliation and anguish of it poured through her like burning acid. She went white with shock and pain, wrenching her arm away from him as she stammered wretchedly, 'No... What happened between us happened...but it won't happen again. I want to make that completely clear to you. *You* may make a habit of indulging in casual sex,' she told him bravely, throwing all restraint aside, 'but I can assure you that *I* do not.'

'Because you're in love with your fiancé.'

His question threw her. She stared at him for a moment and then said quickly, 'Yes...No...That is, I wouldn't indulge in casual sex even if I weren't engaged——' She broke off, biting her bottom lip, and then said huskily and truthfully, 'I can't explain why...what happened between us did happen.'

She swallowed, suddenly feeling drained and defeated, and was stunned to hear him saying softly, almost gently, as though he was trying to reassure her, 'You were missing your fiancé, you were lonely...confused... Tell me about him. What does he look like?'

Emily blinked, thrown into complete confusion. What *did* Travis look like? She tried to remember, and managed to stammer awkwardly, 'Well, he's tall...and blond...'

'You'll have to show me his photograph. You do have a photograph of him, don't you?'

Her mouth dropped. Of course she didn't. At her side, Matt was saying helpfully, 'I only mention it in case I'm likely to meet him.'

'No...no you won't,' Emily told him quickly, tensing when he took hold of her left hand and said quietly, 'You don't wear his ring.'

'No...no...there hasn't been time yet. We only told my parents a little while ago. Travis had to go home to tell *his* parents. No one else in the family knows.'

'He's gone home, without *you*?'

Why was he asking her all these questions, pushing her, making her tell him more and more lies? 'I—I couldn't really go. There's Uncle John's book... Look, I must go downstairs—the dinner——'

'Such reluctance to talk about the man you love. Most women like nothing more, especially when they're newly engaged.'

'Well, I'm not most women,' Emily told him sharply, finally finding the strength to hurry away from him.

'No,' he agreed under his breath, watching her walk stiffly towards the stairs. 'You certainly aren't.'

He was frowning as he walked into his room, recalling the small, betraying stain he had found on his sleeping-bag. It had stunned him with disbelief at first, reinforcing his own crazy feeling that what had happened between them was no casual, meaningless encounter, but something special...something rare...something almost predestined. And then to discover that the woman who had given herself to him so passionately, so completely, had been a virgin and he her first lover. Impossible, surely. But the evidence was there.

He had begun to wish more than ever that he had not let her walk away from him. But he had been so stunned by his own reaction to her, so overwhelmed by the intensity of his desire to make her stay, so caught up in the shocking reality of his own emotions, that she had been gone before he could think of protesting.

And then, when it was too late, he had realised that where an experienced woman, confident enough of herself and her sexuality to indulge so carelessly and passionately in sex with a stranger, might just be able to walk away from what had happened without giving their intimacy a second thought, a virgin, a woman who had had no previous lover, a woman who for whatever reason had never allowed her body to experience whatever need had driven her into his arms, was scarcely capable of the same dispassionate detachment; and, if he had not wanted to find her for his own sake, he must surely then have wanted to find her for her own, to make sure that she was all right . . . that she was not suffering any emotional or psychological scars from what they had shared.

He had tried to trace her, once he was free of the formalities of taking up his new temporary post, going back to the town where he had left her to check up at the garages there, but it had seemed that none of them had dealt with the removal and repair of her car. Having drawn a blank there, he had had to hurry back to Oxford before he could widen his net still further—to try to find a way of curing himself of what he had been feeling over a long period of sleepless nights, when all he could think about was how she had felt in his arms.

Looking at it dispassionately, it wasn't hard to guess why she was so scared. She must be petrified that this fiancé of hers would discover what she had done, presuming of course that he knew she was a virgin. He scowled suddenly. She had claimed that she and this Travis were lovers, but of course that was simply to deceive him. He had seen the terror in her eyes, the fear that he would betray her. His scowl deepened. Just what sort of man did she think he was?

And as for this fiancé of hers . . . didn't he realise how much she needed him with her? Didn't he realise how easily he could lose her? Didn't he care?

He certainly hadn't cared enough to make love to her. The thought slid into his mind like a serpent. He shook his head like a swimmer trying to clear water from his eyes, as he tried to cope with the complexity of his thoughts and feelings.

He was in danger of falling desperately in love with a woman he had only met once, a woman moreover who was in love with and engaged to another man, a woman who had given herself to him so sweetly and so wantonly that the memory of how she had felt in his arms still stirred his senses and his body.

She was plainly terrified of her fiancé discovering what had happened. She must love the man...little though he obviously deserved that love.

Fate had thrown them together once, and now it had chosen to throw them together a second time. Was it—was it really a piece of deliberate self-deception on his part to allow himself to think that two such chance meetings must be more than mere coincidence, that perhaps...

That perhaps what? That she would break her engagement and turn to him? It shocked him to discover how much that thought pleased him... How much he wanted to feel her in his arms again, to hold her, to love her... What was happening to him? When Jolie had deceived him, he had decided grimly that no woman would ever do so again, and yet here he was, virtually on the point of admitting that he wanted a woman who was engaged to someone else. He ought to despise her, not want her.

Perhaps if she hadn't been engaged... But she was, and it went against every principle he had for him to want a woman who was already committed to another man. Emotionally committed, maybe—but sexually...

Sexually she had turned to him, as a substitute for her fiancé. The fiancé who she had claimed was already her lover—but he knew otherwise. If she had lied about that, couldn't she have lied about her reasons for making love with him?

He was clutching at straws, he told himself grimly, looking for something that didn't exist. At least, not on her part.

Hadn't he learned his lesson the first time? Hadn't he learned then that the female sex was possessed of a natural facility for deceit?

But she had seemed so different, he reflected broodingly; in his arms she had made him feel... She had made him feel what? That their coming together, unconventional, reckless though it might have been, had been brought about by a force too strong for either of them to withstand? Daydreams...fantasy...fiction... If he had thought there was something special, something rare and to be treasured about what they had shared, then she had not shared that feeling. For her he had simply been a physical substitute for another man.

A man who she had claimed to him was her lover, when he knew quite categorically that he was not. Why had she lied about that?

CHAPTER FIVE

DOWNSTAIRS in the kitchen, Emily tried to concentrate on the final preparations for dinner, but her mind refused to stay on what she was doing.

Matt, here. She started to tremble and had to replace the heavy saucepan. Why—why had fate decreed such a horrible coincidence?

Just once, once in her life she had behaved in a way that was totally out of character, and look what had happened. Other people did things that were far more reckless than what she had done; other people behaved foolishly, dangerously, and got away with it. But when she did something against all her beliefs, both moral and emotional, far from getting away with it, far from being able to push the entire incident to the back of her mind, with a shudder of relief that she had escaped unscathed, she was confronted by her partner in that shockingly wanton intimacy and forced to live side by side with him in her uncle's home. Forced into fresh deceit in order to protect herself from the consequences of her stupidity.

Had he really imagined that she would be willing to enter into a casual sexual liaison with him? His conversation had indicated as much. Hot, shaming colour stung her face, and her hands trembled as she picked up the saucepan. It was entirely her own fault if he had drawn the wrong conclusions about her. Their coming together, so unexpected, so intense, so almost magical when viewed from the distance that now separated her from it, had taken on in her memories and emotions an almost fairytale-like quality, as though it had been something special, something predestined, a special gift which fate had given her. Maybe they had not loved one another—how could they without any knowledge of one another? But there *had* been tenderness in his hands on her body; his desire had been warmed and softened by that tenderness and by his consideration of her and her own needs, and she in turn had felt such awe, such pleasure when she had touched him that it had been as though she had been waiting for him all her life. Thus she had reasoned that, although what she had done went against all her strongest beliefs, it had somehow been a rare and special experience which had enriched her whole life.

Now, though, those rosy veils of self-deceit had been ripped from her, and she was forced to confront the truth. She had allowed a total stranger to make love to her without giving a single thought for what she was doing. She had thought naïvely, once she knew she wasn't pregnant, that she had nothing further to worry about. How wrong she had been.

Bitterly she wondered what her great-uncle would think if he knew the truth about the man he had welcomed into his home. How many other women had there been before her with whom Matt had shared similar encounters?

Nausea burned her stomach, making her shudder. It was no use trying to convince herself that she had been an innocent victim. She had gone willingly enough into his arms. It was no wonder he had assumed that she would be equally willing to do so again.

If she hadn't pretended that Travis was her fiancé... Her conscience niggled at her. She hated lies and deceit—but what choice had she had? Even so, the momentary look of shocked bitterness in his eyes when she had announced her engagement had caught her off guard and made her wonder if, after all...

If what? If he shared her own ridiculous memories of those hours they had spent together—hours when reality had been suspended and for that short space of time they had forged a bond, shared a rapport, known something so rare and precious that the mere memory of it would warm the coldest days of her life?

How ridiculous she was being. He had shown her the real nature of their intimacy; and if she found that reality bitter and unacceptable then that was *her* fault and not his.

Food was the very last thing she wanted, she recognised half an hour later, toying with her meal while her uncle talked animatedly to Matt. Of the three of them, only her uncle seemed to be really enjoying his meal. He was basically very much a man of his age and upbringing, treating her sex with courtly politeness and warmth and finding only in male company the mental stimulation which was now bringing a sparkle of keenness to his eyes as he talked enthusiastically to Matt about his own years as a don.

Listening to them, Emily realised that Matt had once been one of her great-uncle's students and that it had been her great-uncle who had recommended that he be approached to fill the Chair which had recently become empty. Emily knew that Matt was young to be chosen to fill such a post, and, no matter what his morals might be, as an academic he must be brilliant.

He was certainly tactful, she acknowledged, watching, as he listened to her great-uncle, adding only the odd comment to the conversation. He seemed to understand and accept the older man's need to talk, in no way appearing irritated at his domination of the conversation.

Emily's previous experience of her uncle's fellow dons was that they were in the main an ego-ridden species, rather like a clutch of self-orientated young children in their need to outdo one another.

Once, forgetting for a second her own miseries, she happened to glance at Matt while her uncle was discoursing on one of his pet, and rather outdated educational theories. No touch of boredom shadowed Matt's concentration as he listened to the older man. Instead she saw respect, touched with understanding and humour, and something deep inside her seemed to contract achingly as though someone had gently touched a sensitive spot and brought to life an alien flutter of emotion.

She quelled it immediately. Why, if he had to reappear in her life, destroying her peace of mind, making her confront her own actions and feelings, couldn't Matt behave in such a way as to make it easy for her to feel contempt and dislike for him, instead of one moment filling her with fear and dislike and the next so unexpectedly showing her

gentleness and compassion that he left her feeling
utterly confused and helpless?

Why did fate have to intervene so unkindly in
her life and give her this unwanted insight into his
personality, showing her a man mature enough,
caring enough, to recognise the small vanities of an
older, and probably less able colleague, and to tact-
fully and generously help to preserve them?

She got up from the table almost clumsily,
causing both her uncle and Matt to look up at her.
Her uncle, she saw, was frowning vaguely, as
though he had forgotten she was there.

'I wanted to do some more work on your notes,
Uncle John,' she told him, deliberately avoiding
looking at Matt. 'I'll take your coffee through into
the study for you, shall I?'

'Yes, a marvellous idea.'

Matt was standing up, walking over to the door
and opening it for her, she recognised numbly. She
had no alternative but to walk towards him, her
whole body tensing almost to the point where it
was impossible to move, as she finally stood within
inches of him and the sanctuary of the open door.

'That was a lovely meal,' he told her quietly.
'While you're making the coffee, perhaps I could
clear the table for you.'

Emily couldn't quite hide her surprise. She gave
him a quick, startled glance that betrayed how
unused she was to such consideration. If they hadn't
already met—if she hadn't already known... If they
were in truth strangers, just by watching him and
listening to him tonight she must have been in intense danger of—of what? Falling in love with him?

That was the kind of thing teenagers did, not grown women.

Her uncle had turned round, to see what was delaying Matt's return to the table. 'I was just offering to repay your niece's wonderful cooking by helping with the washing-up,' he explained easily.

'Good heavens, no—there's no need for that,' Uncle John told him before Emily could speak. 'That's women's stuff, my dear boy. Best leave Emily to get on with it. Very good at that sort of thing, my niece.'

Emily saw the way Matt frowned, the look of disdain that darkened his eyes for a moment as he looked at her uncle.

'Actually, I *do* prefer to wash this particular dinner service on my own,' she said quickly. 'It's very old and very fragile, and I need my full concentration to make sure none of it gets damaged.' Something she wouldn't have a hope of giving the washing-up with Matt standing by.

She could see that Matt's mouth was still compressed, as though he wanted to argue the matter further, but it was only when she had actually escaped to the kitchen that it struck her that this offer might not have been as altruistic as it had appeared. That perhaps he had wanted to get her on her own so that he could . . .

What? Persuade her to go to bed with him? When she had first met him, his straggly beard and unkempt appearance had hidden the truth from her, and that truth was that Matt Slater was an extremely attractive man, the kind of man that few women would be able to resist. She was quite sure that if he wanted a sexual partner he would have very little difficulty in finding one. Of course, she was here on the spot, and it would be very difficult for him to invite a woman to spend the night with him while he was living here with her uncle. But tonight, listening to him, he hadn't come across as a man so unable to control his physical needs that they would drive him to propositioning a woman who had made it plain that she did not want a sexual liaison with him.

And she had made it plain that she did not. But hadn't she also previously equally intensely given him the impression that, not only was she sexually available, but also that she was sexually eager and desirous of making love with him.

When she took the coffee into the study, both men were deep in conversation, but that didn't stop Matt from getting up and taking the tray from her. For a brief second of time his fingers touched hers, an electrical contact that twisted her stomach in knots of frightened acknowledgement of how much that touch affected her.

She was trembling when she escaped from the room, as much from the shock that that jolting surge of awareness had given her as from the stripping, caustic look Matt had given her. It was as though, in that short space of time, he had looked into her soul and seen what only *she* had the right to know lay there; as though he had confronted her mentally and emotionally, demanding that she acknowledge her reaction to him.

But why? Male pride? Physical desire?

She tried to dismiss both Matt and her own re-action to him from her mind as she washed up. It was true that washing the valuable china did re-

quire complete concentration. It took her a long
time to complete her task and put everything away;
so long in fact that, instead of going into her small
office to work as she had planned, she decided she
might as well go straight to bed.

None of the rooms in the old-fashioned house
had their own private bathrooms, something which
had never bothered her in the past since her great-
uncle used the bathroom closest to his room, and
she used another at the other end of the landing;
but Matt's room lay in between the two bathrooms, and she couldn't help wishing that it were
possible for her to undress and use the bathroom,
all within the privacy of her closed bedroom door,
rather than having to walk down the landing
wearing her old towelling robe.

But when half an hour later she opened her
bedroom door, she found the landing reassuringly
empty; the two men were obviously still downstairs
talking.

How very indicative of the differing attitudes of
men and women to the kind of intimacy she and
Matt had shared it was that, while she hadn't
stopped agonising over the incident since the
moment she had opened the front door and seen
Matt standing there, he seemed to have no problem
at all in dismissing the whole thing from his mind
and spending the evening listening to her uncle's
conversation with every evidence of relaxation and
enjoyment.

The landing was still empty when she opened the
bathroom door a little later; she might have been
completely alone in the house. Beneath her fear,
her anguish and the loss of her self-respect lay an

odd strand of sensation she couldn't entirely analyse, and it was only later when she was lying in bed trying to sleep, but in reality tensing, waiting for the sounds that would herald Matt's arrival upstairs, that she managed to isolate and recognise that odd sensation for what it was.

When she did, a sharp shrill of self-disgust coiled through her. Disappointment! How *could* she possibly feel disappointed? She didn't *want* Matt to think she was sexually available, did she? She didn't *want* him to believe that he could casually resume the intensely intimate relationship they had shared for those few brief hours? Of course she didn't. So why was she feeling like this—*why* was her memory playing tricks on her by causing her to recall the delicious safe, warm, loved sensation she had experienced held in Matt's arms?

Loved—what nonsense; Matt hadn't loved her, nor she him. What was the matter with her? Was she so unable to face up to the unpalatable reality of her own behaviour that she was now seeking to cloak it in some shadowing protective cloak of emotion, trying to pretend that there had been more to it than a mere sexual coming together?

Angrily she turned over on to her stomach, trying to dismiss the alien emotions and feelings crowding her brain and body. She didn't want Matt here, invading her life, disturbing her peace, forcing her into deceit. She didn't want him reminding her of what she had done, and most of all she didn't want him here because of the way he made her feel, both about herself and about him.

She was a fool, she derided herself silently. A woman who gave herself sexually to a stranger because she had suddenly and inescapably realised that life was passing her by. And then she had compounded that folly by weaving idiotic, impossible daydreams around him, so that, when she was confronted by the reality of him, he had torn through the delicate, clouding veils of self-protection she had thrown up around herself and her actions, making her see what had happened with all the stark bleakness of that reality. He had taken away from her her sheltering, protective dreams; had stripped their coming together of the soft romanticism in which she had shrouded it, with his careless assumption that she would be happy to enter into a relationship with him based entirely on sexual need.

It had shocked her how much that had hurt, so that in that one split second she had realised how far she had actually allowed herself to travel down a road which she had had no right to enter at all.

From that one brief union they had shared, she had started to build up a store of fantasy, of 'maybe's, of impossible dreams, all the more comforting because they had been impossible. Now those dreams had been completely destroyed and it was no longer possible for her to cloak the raw reality of what she had done with the saving grace of imagined mutual caring and respect, with the tiny seeds of hope and tenderness which, carefully cherished, might have one day turned into love.

So she had comforted and consoled herself, free to put the incident safely behind her and to allow herself the luxury of pretending that given different circumstances, more space, more time, they might just possibly have established a proper relationship.

Now all that was gone. To Matt she had simply been a willing, anonymous partner in the sexual act they had shared. He was quite willing to extend that partnership, as he had made plain, but she was filled with revulsion at the thought of what she had done, of how she had broken all her own rules and beliefs.

It was a long time before she finally dropped off to sleep.

'You won't forget that the publisher is coming to see you this afternoon, will you, Uncle John?' Emily reminded her relative.

They had just finished breakfast. Matt had gone upstairs to collect some papers. Her uncle was going with him to his college and, knowing how quickly Uncle John lost all track of time once he was with his cronies, Emily had taken the opportunity of reminding him of his afternoon appointment.

'No, I shan't forget. While he's here, I'm hoping that Matt will have time to read through the manuscript. I'd value his opinion. By the way, that young man who telephoned you last night——'

'It wasn't anything important, Uncle John,' Emily responded quickly. 'Will you be in for dinner tonight?'

'No. We'll both be dining at High Table. Now, what time did you say that young man was coming to see me?'

'Two-thirty,' Emily replied patiently, one eye on the kitchen door as she waited for Matt to reappear, her stomach twisted in knots of tension.

And yet, for all her anguish and self-criticism, breakfast had not been the ordeal she had anticipated. In fact, if she hadn't known just how Matt regarded her, she would have been completely deceived by his manner towards her.

This morning, for instance, he had insisted that she sit down and finish her own breakfast, and that he make the fresh pot of tea her uncle had requested. Before she could protest he had been out of his chair, filling the kettle.

And then after breakfast he had thanked her so warmly, so caringly almost, as though it concerned him that the management of the household fell on her shoulders.

Although she was always an early riser, she had been surprised to find him coming in from the garden when she had gone downstairs dressed in her customary uniform of plain brown skirt and an equally dull shirt and jumper.

'That's a wonderful garden you've got out there,' he had commented as easily as though they were indeed strangers.

'It's rather overgrown, I'm afraid,' had been her stilted reply. 'I just don't get the time.'

'No. Well, perhaps while I'm here your uncle will allow me to indulge my back-to-nature instincts and do some work on it.'

He had brought into the kitchen with him the cool, sharp scent of the early morning, and without even knowing she was doing it she had been drawn closer towards him, so that abruptly and shockingly she had suddenly realised she was within touching distance of his fingertips. She had taken a step backwards then, saying jerkily that she must take her uncle a cup of tea otherwise he would wonder what had happened to her.

'I thought you worked here as his researcher-cum-assistant,' he had challenged her almost angrily. 'Not as his housekeeper.'

'I enjoy looking after him,' she had retaliated defensively, keeping her back to him, her body stiff with the resentment and bitterness of all the years of listening to her parents' bewilderment at this totally alien urge to nurture she seemed to possess. 'Some people do, you know. I find nothing demeaning or menial in wanting to provide someone with a comfortable home. Not every human being wants to strive for academic or material success; we don't *all* want to climb mountains and conquer the world, and it infuriates me that, just because we don't want these things, we're constantly made to feel that we're some sort of sub-species.'

He said quietly, 'I quite agree. There's a very special satisfaction to be found in discovering and recognising one's talents and in finding the most satisfying way of utilising them. Contentment is a state of mind that far too few people really value as they ought, although of course in this day and age your sex is often forced to take on the triple role of wife, mother and contributor to the family income as well.'

'You mean, not all women are allowed the luxury of indulging their desire to nurture? Well, I know how lucky I am.'

'And your fiancé, does he know how fortunate he is, I wonder?'

The soft-voiced question had completely silenced her. She had been so determined to defend herself from what she had seen as his criticism of her way of life—the same kind of criticism she had received so often from her family and friends—that she had completely forgotten everything else. She had stared at him, unaware of the confusion darkening her eyes and the way they were suddenly shadowed with fear.

What was the matter with the man, Matt had wondered bitterly, that he could induce such uncertainty and low self-esteem in the woman he proclaimed he loved? What was their relationship based on, that she had felt the need to lose herself and her innocence in his arms?

He had turned away from her so abruptly that Emily had thought he must have somehow or other divined that tiny betraying twist of sensation inside her; that he must have known of that idiotic, helpless yearning deep inside her, impelling her to move closer to him even while she had remained frozen where she stood, immobilised by the strength of what she had been feeling. And then he had been gone, striding through the kitchen, leaving her to come back to reality and to wish that she had never, ever met him.

Now, as soon as she heard the sound of him coming downstairs, she turned her back towards the kitchen door, busying herself with a small, unnecessary task, so that there was no need for her to do anything other than throw a stiff 'goodbye' over her shoulder to them as he and her uncle made their departure.

With him gone, she knew she ought to have felt easier, better—that she ought to have been able to shut herself away in her small office and concentrate on her work. She ought to have been, but she was sitting staring unseeing into space far more than she ought to, she recognised.

CHAPTER SIX

SINCE this wasn't one of the days when Mrs Beattie came to help in the house, once the men had gone Emily had plenty to do before she could shut herself away in her small office and get to work on Uncle John's notes.

As she went upstairs to clean the bedrooms and bathrooms, she knew how irritated both her parents would be if they could see what she was doing. At home order was only imposed on the chaos of her parents' household by Louise. Her parents, so untidy and uncaring at home, though, were strict disciplinarians when it came to preparing for their travels; she knew that her mother especially found it extremely difficult to understand how any daughter of hers could actually enjoy housework, and Emily had always felt as though in doing so she was letting her down in some way.

She remembered how when, as a child she had asked one Christmas for a doll, her mother had gently tried to persuade her to have something else instead.

For a time she had striven to match her parents' way of life, but she hated travelling, hated not having a home...roots. She loved the mental stimulation of working on her uncle's book, but she also found pleasure in polishing the house's old furniture, in cooking meals, in arranging the wind and rain-damaged flowers she rescued from the garden.

Her uncle left his bedroom and bathroom in a state of wild disorder; but, to Emily's surprise, when she walked cautiously into Matt's room, having stood outside the closed door for a good ten minutes giving herself a firm talking to, and telling herself that she must look on him as nothing more than another colleague of her uncle's, she discovered that, not only was the bed neatly made, but also that everything in the room was as pin-neat as it had been before Matt moved in.

Only a jacket lying casually on the back of the armchair testified to the fact that the room was occupied. Automatically she walked towards it and picked it up. It was the same jacket he had worn that fatal night when they had met—she was sure of it.

Its familiar scent of worn, soft leather enveloped her so that, without knowing she was doing so, her fingers curled tightly into the worn fabric, as though it gave her some support. Memories, so sharply clear, so shockingly wanton, so intensely real that she could even feel their echo in the immediate physical reaction of her body, swamped her.

Now, when it was far, far too late for her to do anything about it, she recognised that the impetuosity, the need, the intensity which had carried her past the barriers of self-restraint and caution had had nothing to do with the fact that Gracie was engaged, nor with the fact that at twenty-six she had never had a lover. Against all the odds, against everything she had believed about herself, she had looked at Matt and subconsciously she had wanted *him*, not just a man but one particular man: *Matt*.

She had wanted Matt. She sat down unsteadily on the bed, still clutching the jacket. But she had never wanted a man. Not like that...not so intensely, so sharply, so achingly that that wanting had been stronger than any other feeling she had ever experienced, even with Gerry.

She drew a deep, shuddering breath. Outside, a skittish breeze blew the branches of the stately magnolia against the window. In a few months, those bare branches would be a mass of glorious, deep pink, cup-shaped flowers. In a few months, the overgrown herbaceous borders would be a tangled mass of columbines, trumpet flowers and rose campions. In a few months, Matt would be gone and she would be able to return to her safe, protected world. She would be free from these ridiculous tormenting thoughts, from this dangerous need to investigate every thought and feeling she had.

So what if she *had* felt desire for Matt—she was human, wasn't she? She got up, pacing the room tensely, still clutching the jacket. She was *allowed* to have normal human feelings, wasn't she—normal human failings? Countless numbers of her sex did exactly what she had done without suffering for it the way she was now suffering.

She could hardly bring herself to look at her own reflection in the mirror without wincing. It had been bad enough before, when she had only had her own knowledge of what she had done to contend with, but now there was Matt—a man who knew more about her than any other human being, a man who had seen her stripped of the comfortable clothing of civilisation, who had seen her defenceless and unprotected.

Was that why she felt so tense and afraid? Because she felt in some way that in giving herself to Matt she had exposed herself to him in a way that would always make her vulnerable?

If only he wasn't here; if only she had never had to see him again, she would have been able to cope, to put the incident behind her, to bury it decently and completely. Now it was beginning to haunt her... Just as Matt had haunted her dreams ever since that night.

She was standing in front of the window, staring out of it without seeing the view. In her mind's eye she was back in the Land Rover with Matt, wrapped in his arms, loving the sensation of his bare flesh against her own, aching for the soft drift of his hands against her body... his body against...

With a low tormented cry she dropped the jacket, closing her eyes as she leaned her hot face against the cool glass. What on earth was happening to her? Why was she doing this to herself? She ought to remember what had happened with loathing and disgust, not with this aching yearning, this wanton flowering of sensation, this physical and emotional loneliness that swelled and ached inside her and made her eyes and throat sting with silly, useless tears.

Crying—over Matt... Why, for goodness' sake? Why was she letting her subconscious weave these idiotic, dangerous daydreams around him, turning him from a man who had simply made the most of the opportunity she had so foolishly given him to indulge his sexual appetite into an imaginary creature of tenderness and compassion, into a fictional sharer with her in a coming together that had held the promise of far more than a merely physical joining of their bodies.

Why was she allowing herself to torment herself like this? Was it because she couldn't bear to accept that she could desire someone so intensely without feeling any emotion for them? Was she now trying to convince herself that she had felt some emotion for Matt?

If so, she was an even greater fool to herself than she had ever imagined, she told herself as she went back downstairs. There was far more danger in emotionally wanting Matt than there had ever been in simply physically wanting him.

Confused by her own thoughts and needs, she wandered out into the garden. Here, strangely, her orderly mind found something special and pleasurable in looking at the wild havoc that nature, left to her own devices, had created here. She liked the overgrown borders and tangled climbers, the fruit trees which produced vast quantities of blossom but precious little fruit. Only really in the vegetable garden did she yearn to see order restored and production recommenced.

Her pots of herbs stood in the shelter of the kitchen garden wall. The wind tugged at soft strands of her hair, dragging it loose from her neat chignon. She ought to be inside, making her uncle's favourite fruit-bread for this afternoon, not mooning around out here dreaming impossible and dangerous dreams.

Sighing faintly, she went back to the house, letting its ancient silence wrap itself around her, but for once she didn't find the silence soothing. Instead, as she prepared the moist tea-bread her uncle loved, she found her mind drifting off at a tangent, peopling the large kitchen with children—dark-haired, blue-eyed, with quick intelligent faces and their father's curling, heart-stopping smile.

Her whole body went still. Long, long ago, when Gerry had stripped the scales of self-delusion from her eyes and had made her see herself as the rest of his sex saw her, she had put away the daydreams of her growing years: of a husband, children, the kind of domestic happiness she had yearned for so much herself as a child, all those years when she had been growing up and her parents had been exuberant, awe-inspiring strangers who had swooped on her at odd intervals making her feel both excited and nervous at the same time, so that it was almost a relief when they had disappeared again.

She had learned then to keep to herself her unfashionable dreams of domesticity, but still they had persisted, flourishing in the secret places of her heart. It had taken Gerry's cruelty to finally banish them and to make her focus her life in another direction.

Second-best—a lukewarm marriage bereft of the passion and intensity she had ached for so much—would never be enough to fill the empty yearning she had inside. She had thought she had come to accept reality, to be content with what life had given her, and now, cruelly and surely unnecessarily, fate had decided to taunt her with all that she could never have.

Such thoughts were not only unproductive but dangerous as well, she told herself firmly, the bread made, the kitchen tidy, and the work she had left in the study demanding her attention. Firmly refusing to allow herself to give in to any more self-indulgence, she started work.

The publisher was due at half-past two, and she only hoped that her uncle would return in time to meet him. Brilliant though he was in his chosen field, when it came to more mundane matters her uncle was hopelessly vague.

At two o'clock, she carefully stacked her typewritten sheets of paper and cleared her desk. Then she went upstairs, washed her face and brushed her hair into its neat bob before carefully applying the small amount of make-up Gracie had long ago persuaded her to wear.

'You're so fair-skinned,' Gracie had told her doubtful sister. 'You really do need some colour. It needn't look heavy and overdone.' And Emily had to admit that the soft blusher, the subtle smoky eyeshadow, the mascara and the pretty lipstick did add a certain definition to her face.

Applying them, she told herself stoutly that Matt's arrival had nothing to do with the fact that she was taking extra special care with her appearance—far from it. The last thing she wanted was to attract the attention of a man who had already made it plain that all he wanted from her was a willing sexual partner. There was nothing wrong in wanting to make a good impression on her great-uncle's publisher, she told herself quickly as her hand hesitated. Nothing wrong at all. After all, just because she enjoyed the kind of work and lifestyle that so many of her contemporaries scorned, it did not mean that she had to behave and look like some kind of dowdy little mouse.

She wasn't beautiful, it was true, but Gracie was right—the make-up did add a subtle definition to her face, the eyeshadow did draw attention to the smoky prettiness of her eyes, the mascara did emphasise eyelashes which were surprisingly thick and long.

Perhaps it was this that led her to changing into the unusual green-blue tartan kilt that her parents had bought her for Christmas and the sunshine-yellow sweater that went with it, matching the pretty over-lining of yellow that highlighted the kilt.

The outfit was far more fashionable and colourful than anything she would have chosen for herself, but as she studied her reflection she decided defiantly that she was going to wear it. With a very un-Emily-like toss of her hair, she hurried downstairs to prepare the tray for the substantial afternoon tea she knew that Uncle John would expect her to serve to his guest.

This took longer than she had expected, and she was just carrying the tray through into the study when she heard the sound of a car outside and then Matt and her uncle walking into the hall.

Her stomach muscles knotted as she heard them walking towards the open study door. Perhaps Matt would go straight upstairs and not bother to come in, she told herself, her body unconsciously defensive as she stood facing the door, standing ramrod-straight, her chin lifting defiantly.

'Ah, good, you've made the tea,' her uncle said as he walked in. 'That wind is surprisingly cold. I take it our visitor hasn't arrived as yet?'

'He's not due until two-thirty,' Emily responded automatically. For some reason she was finding it impossible to remove her gaze from Matt. He was standing framed in the doorway, simply watching her in a sober, unfathomable way that made her heart skip and her pulse race.

Her uncle was still talking, but Emily had lost the ability to concentrate on anything other than Matt. Her mouth went dry, and she felt herself trembling inwardly.

'I'd better go and fill the kettle,' she heard herself saying mundanely. What was the matter with her? Why did he provoke this powerful and dangerous awareness?

'Yes—and you might bring another cup, Emily. I'd like Matt to join us. He's had experience of this kind of thing.'

'Not much,' Matt said self-deprecatingly. 'Some small articles, and a text-book. Nothing like this.'

Although he was speaking to her uncle, he was still looking at her. Why? Why deliberately try to make her feel uncomfortable? Unless, like her, he was physically incapable of looking away. Unless, like her... Her heart gave a tremendous jump, she felt both sick and excited at the same time. Stop it, she told herself sternly. Stop imagining things that don't exist. You know what kind of man he really is. You know what he really wants from you.

It was like suddenly coming down to earth after floating with the clouds—a jolting, sickening sensation that caused real physical pain to grip her stomach. She found as she managed to drag her gaze away from him that she was actually shaking with nervous strain. When he didn't move away from the door until she was almost abreast of it, her stomach lurched betrayingly.

'I'll come and help you with the tea,' he offered courteously.

It was impossible for her to speak. She simply shook her head and almost ran past him into the kitchen, closing the door behind her and leaning on it for several seconds until she felt able to walk slowly and carefully over to the kettle.

She heard the sound of a second car arriving while she was making the tea, and then the sound of firm decisive footsteps crossing the hall. Matt had obviously heard the car as well and had gone to let the publisher in.

She would give the men a few minutes to introduce themselves and get settled, she decided, but only seconds had actually passed when the kitchen door opened and Matt came in.

'He's arrived,' he told her.

'Yes, I know.' She gave him a tight, strained smile as she turned round. 'I'll bring the tea in in a second,' she added dismissively—but he refused to be dismissed, staying where he was, watching her intently.

'What a creature of disguises you are,' he said softly at last. 'The night we met, you were the epitome of the modern, free-thinking woman who makes her own rules for the way she lives her life. Then last night, so demure, all neutral, disguising colours; and now today yet another Emily. No need to ask whose benefit this one is for,' he added acidly. 'I'm sure he'll be impressed by you, Emily. He looks the kind who likes his women ladylike but not too demure. The way you've got your hair soft and free like that should really turn him on...make him wonder what it would be like to slide his fingers through it and use its soft delicacy to hold you captive under his mouth. And I'm sure he's going to enjoy the way that deceptively prim and proper sweater you're wearing hints so cleverly at the femininity of the body it conceals. There's something about the soft thrust of a woman's breasts beneath a slightly oversized fine wool sweater that's covertly erotic... But then, *I* don't need to tell you that, do I?' he added smoothly. 'I'm sure your fiancé has already told you as much and far more.'

He was angry with her, Emily recognised as her stunned brain tried to make sense of the patently ridiculous accusations he was throwing at her.

'What is it exactly that you want from my sex, Emily?' he grated, immobilising her with apprehension as he took a step towards her and then another. Heavens—he was so large, so tall and masculinely threatening in a way that made her stomach go weak with a sensation which shamingly wasn't entirely fear.

'You're engaged, and yet you gave yourself to me when——' Matt broke off abruptly, fighting to control the emotions rioting inside him.

What on earth was the matter with him? Just because he had discovered that he was a woman's first lover, that was no reason for him to develop this crazy, almost possessive attitude towards her. She was engaged to someone else, for heaven's sake.

But it had been to him she had turned for physical intimacy, for passion. To *him*!

His silence enabled Emily to break out of the trance he seemed to have put her in, and reach for the tea-tray. Inwardly she was still shaking with tension and reaction, but she wasn't going to let him see how much his anger had affected her.

Head held high, she carried the tray towards the open door, ignoring Matt's muttered, 'I'll carry that for you.'

Out in the hallway, unable to resist the impulse to glance at herself in the mirror, she saw that her colour was unusually high and, shockingly, that the yellow jumper did, as Matt had described, somehow give subtle emphasis to the gentle swell of her breasts in a way that might just perhaps be described as provocative.

Provocative. She had never done anything remotely needing that description in her life. She had not even bought the jumper, she wanted to tell him, never mind put it on for the reasons he had so humiliatingly described. It had never, ever occurred to her to wear anything to deliberately draw attention to her body; she had never thought it particularly worthy of drawing attention to. And yet Matt had noticed it—had noticed and cruelly and inaccurately accused her of deliberate wantonness.

The teapot and hot-water jug chinked noisily as her hands trembled. Somehow or other Matt had reached the study door ahead of her, and, when he opened it for her, either by accident or design he held it open in such a way that her body had to brush dangerously close to his as she passed through the opening. Immediately her flesh broke out in a rash of goosebumps, a *frisson* of sensation making her shiver visibly, so that both Matt, and the man standing next to her uncle apparently deep in conversation with him, both focused on her.

The quick, assessing male interest that sparkled momentarily in the publisher's eyes startled her so much that Emily simply stared back at him. What on earth had happened to her? What had changed her from being a woman she could have sworn that no man glanced at with any degree of sexual interest, into someone who merited those discreet but very definitely interested male appraisals that both Matt and the publisher had given her?

It couldn't have anything to do with the fact that she and Matt had made love, could it? Automatically she gnawed anxiously on her bottom lip, telling herself that she was being an idiot; that, to put it bluntly, the fact that she was no longer a virgin was hardly something discernible to the naked eye. No, the difference must spring from her—be caused by something within her...her hands shook as she put down the tray. She didn't like the idea that her body might be indiscreetly and flagrantly inviting men to find it sexually interesting without the knowledge of her mind.

As she put down the tray, Matt came forward to help her, but the publisher beat him to it, smiling warmly at her as he introduced himself.

'Your uncle has been telling me how hard you've been working on his book, and that you'll be able to tell me far more about its progress than he can himself. What I liked particularly about it was the human aspect of its characters. When it first arrived, I was expecting the traditional kind of learned work-form we expect to receive from a man of your uncle's erudition. To find something so refreshing and readable came as a complete surprise. We're very keen to publish.'

Emily was blushing. She couldn't help it. She wondered if Peter Cavendish had guessed that *she* was responsible for the humanising of her uncle's work. She listened guiltily as her uncle and Peter talked, discussing various aspects of the book, with Matt putting in one or two pertinent comments now and again.

Emily busied herself pouring and handing round cups of tea and the small delicate sandwiches her great-uncle liked.

'I understand that you have a degree yourself,' Peter Cavendish commented to her. 'Are you in between career moves at the moment, or...?'

Here it was again, that assumption that she couldn't possibly find satisfaction in the work she was doing, the life she was living—that she must want to be out among the other frantic go-getters, pursuing commercial success.

'I'm not particularly career-orientated,' she said quietly and with dignity. She had no intention of pretending to be something she wasn't, not even with this very charming man who was looking at her in a way that made her wonder if her mother had actually known the effect the yellow jumper was likely to have before she had bought it.

'Maybe not, but you've certainly made an excellent job of interpreting your uncle's work. You've obviously got a gift for this kind of thing, and if you're ever looking for fresh work please get in touch with me and let me know. You'd be a godsend to some of our writers.'

He went on to make several other flattering comments about the standard of her work, leaving Emily feeling surprised and pleased, and when, after his discussions with her uncle had come to an end, he accompanied her back to her own office to talk to her in more detail about the extent of her own contribution to the manuscript, Emily discovered that she had been right in guessing that he had realised that she was responsible for humanising the work.

'I'll be frank with you, if I may,' Peter Cavendish told her, quietly closing the door so that they couldn't be overheard. 'Your uncle is obviously a very learned man, but learned men do not always have the knack of making their pet subjects interesting and therefore readable. This book of your uncle's is different. You're responsible for that, although I suspect your uncle doesn't actually realise it. Does he ever read what you've typed?' he asked her humorously.

Emily flushed. 'Yes, of course he does,' she said defensively.

'Mm... Well, we'd like him to complete the manuscript as quickly as he can. I realise that he does have other commitments, that he is only semi-retired, but do you think that, say, six months would be long enough to complete a first draft?'

Mentally calculating how much work was yet to be done, Emily was concentrating so hard on checking through how much work she actually had in hand and how much still had to be done that she bumped into a large pile of reference books perched on the edge of her desk. As they fell off, Peter Cavendish darted forward, quickly grabbing hold of her and pulling her out of the way of the heavy tomes.

Emily was just thanking him gratefully, conscious of how painful it would have been if the full weight of the books had fallen on to her, when the office door opened abruptly and Matt walked in.

Peter had his arm around her shoulders, his other hand resting lightly on her waist. He had been about to say something to her, and she had turned her face up towards his. There was nothing really intimate about his touch; she might have been any woman he had rescued, but she saw immediately from Matt's face that he had totally misconstrued their closeness.

Immediately she flushed guiltily and pulled away from Peter, even though she knew she had no reason to feel as though she had done anything wrong. And even if Peter had been about to kiss her, as Matt so obviously suspected, it was really no business of his, she told herself indignantly.

'John wanted to go over one or two points again with you,' Matt was saying flatly to Peter, ignoring her completely, Emily recognised.

Inwardly seething, she pretended that she **was** too busy to go back to the study with them. In reality she wanted some time by herself to try to get a grip on her runaway emotions.

Twenty minutes later Peter popped his head around the office door to tell her that he was leaving. 'And remember,' he added, 'if you ever feel like a change of scene, I can think of half a dozen writers who'd jump at the chance of employing you. It can't be much fun for you living and working here with your uncle.'

Wondering what he would say if she told him that she had chosen to work for her uncle, Emily thanked him and said goodbye. She glanced at her watch. It was almost time for her to start the preparations for dinner.

Her uncle and presumably Matt as well had gone outside to see Peter off. While the study was empty she removed the tea trolley and wheeled it into the kitchen, to stack the china in the dishwasher. She was engrossed in this task when the door opened and Matt walked in.

He looked furiously angry, she realised, her heart suddenly plummeting. It was no use telling herself that he had no right to be angry; her body refused to recognise the logic of her mind.

'What is it with you?' he demanded without preamble. 'Does it give you some kind of thrill to pick up strangers and make love with them? Some kind of sexual excitement that you don't get with your fiancé? First me, and now Cavendish.'

Emily had been staring at him in disbelief, unable to comprehend what he was saying to her, unable to understand the accusations he was making, protected from the bitter anger she could hear in his voice by some kind of invisible bubble. But the moment he stopped speaking and reached towards her as though he was going to physically shake her, the bubble broke, exposing her to the most acute physical pain she had ever experienced in her life.

Without stopping to ask herself why it should hurt so much, *why* it should matter so much what Matt thought of her, she tore past him, ignoring his demand that she stop, racing upstairs and not stopping until she had reached the sanctuary of her bedroom.

As she sank down on her bed, she discovered that she was crying—agonised, painful sobs that wrenched from her chest and tore at her throat.

'Emily... I'm sorry, I didn't mean...'

Matt was standing just inside her bedroom, quietly closing the door, watching her, and immediately she was conscious of the picture she must present. She could feel the wetness of her tears streaking her face and glared angrily at him. She wasn't going to wipe them away in front of him. He had no right to follow her into her room. No right to have said the things to her that he had said. No right.

A gleam of sunlight shone through her bedroom window, picking out the tears clinging to her eyelashes. She heard Matt breathe in deeply, and focused automatically on the sharp lifting of his chest. The silence between them was stretched taut with tension. Emily felt as though she needed to gasp for air, as though suddenly it was almost impossible for her to breathe. Her heart was racing far too quickly. Matt's features seemed to dissolve and reshape themselves as she tried to blink away the remainder of her tears. And surely he was much closer to her now than he had been.

She drew in a shaky breath and then another as he came closer to her bed. She had an overpowering desire to back away from him, but she wouldn't let herself give in to it. 'You have no right to be in here,' she told him instead.

'According to you, I have no rights at all where you're concerned, and yet I've been your lover. I've touched your skin, caressed and tasted it; I've felt your body move under mine... I've held you naked in my arms and felt you glory in that nakedness. I've loved you, Emily, and that——'

'Loved me. You mean, you've had sex with me,' she said shrilly. What on earth was he trying to do to her? Why was he saying these things? Why was he tormenting her like this? She knew that all he wanted from her was a resumption of the intimacy they had so briefly shared—but not out of love. She wasn't that much of a fool.

She saw his face change, something hardening in his eyes, but his voice was calm and even as he said quietly, 'Very well then, I've had sex with you...and now I want——'

'And now you want to use me as a sexual convenience,' Emily interrupted him bitterly. 'Well, I won't *be* used in that way, Matt. I may stupidly have once allowed you——'

'Allowed me? You asked me...begged me,' he told her savagely. 'You wanted it as much as I did, you——'

'No...No...No...' Emily moaned covering her ears and shaking her head from side to side, her control broken as the words hit her like physical blows.

'Yes,' Matt insisted, striding over to the bed and taking hold of her wrists to wrench her hands away from her ears. 'Yes,' he repeated with soft emphasis. 'Emily, I——'

He broke off, suddenly silent, the way he was looking at her oddly mesmeric, like the slow caress of his fingers against the fast pulse of her inner wrists. Something was happening to her, something familiar and dangerous—something that only Matt seemed to be able to set in motion.

Once before he had made her feel like this. Once before. But even though her brain shrieked danger, her body refused to listen. Her lips parted, her eyes becoming slumberous and shadowed with memories. The pulse in her wrist hammered wildly beneath his stroking touch.

The soft, almost inaudible murmur Matt made deep in his throat was interpreted faultlessly by her body, so that immediately it softened and yielded, yearning eagerly towards him.

She felt his hands in her hair, moulding the shape of her head, holding her still, his fingers softly caressing as he bent towards her. She knew that he was going to kiss her—knew and did nothing to avoid the fierce male pressure of his mouth. Somehow or other, her arms were already around him, her fingers tracing the hard bones of his shoulders, her eyes closing in eager anticipation of the pleasure to come.

The sound of her uncle's voice calling her name outside her door shocked her back to reality, making her pull back abruptly at the same moment as Matt released her. She couldn't bring herself to look at him, to endure the humiliation of the triumph she knew must be in his eyes.

'Coming, Uncle John,' she called out shakily, sliding off the bed and walking stiffly past Matt without even glancing at him, knowing that, if her uncle hadn't appeared, if they had not been interrupted, she would willingly and wantonly have allowed Matt to press her down against the covers of her bed and make love to her as he had done once before, and that, not only would she have done nothing to stop him, but that she would actively and eagerly have aided and abetted him.

CHAPTER SEVEN

QUITE apart from her own very personal and private reasons for not wanting Matt's presence in her great-uncle's house, his arrival had had an extremely adverse effect on Uncle John's progress with his book, Emily reflected irritably, glaring at her empty desk and pristine-neat study.

Matt had been here for almost two weeks, and during that time her great-uncle had spent far more time either with Matt or at the university than he had done at home.

She couldn't deny that Matt's presence seemed to have given Uncle John a new lease of life and a renewed enthusiasm and zest, but only yesterday Peter Cavendish had telephoned her to check on the progress of the manuscript and she had had to fob him off with a tactful fib.

Today, Matt and Uncle John were lunching with the provost and then this evening they were dining with some fellow dons. Ordinarily Emily would have welcomed the chance to have some time to herself, but, when she ought to have welcomed it even more, finding release from the continual apprehension that stalked her whenever Matt was in the house, she found herself wandering restlessly from room to room until she abruptly realised that she was standing outside Matt's closed bedroom door. What *was* the matter with her? When he had first arrived she had been panicked by his cold-

blooded assumption that she would be willing to
sleep with him; but now, as the days passed, she
found it harder and harder to cling on to the anger
and shock of that moment and instead her mind
kept on returning to their first meeting, to the sensation she had had then that he was a man of strong
character and compassion—a man with whom she
could have had a good deal in common.

With each day that passed, he revealed another
facet of his character to her—a character which she
was gradually forced to accept was strangely at odds
with the impression she had gained on their second
meeting.

Or was she simply deluding herself? Was it all
just a game to him—was he deliberately and cruelly
stalking her, undermining her determination to
stand aloof from him? If so, why? If all he wanted
was a sexual partner, there must be any number of
women who would be only too willing.

Grimly walking away from his door, she wondered if he had realised yet that his greatest ally was
the traitor within herself: her own body, her own
physical responsiveness to him. Or had she misjudged the situation entirely and had he grown
bored with pursuing her?

Certainly, since that afternoon in her bedroom
when he had kissed her so furiously and so
passionately, he had made no further attempt to
touch her. There were times, though, when she
found him watching her with an odd brooding intensity that made her stomach churn.

Outwardly he was everything she had ever
dreamed of in the man she could love: caring, com-
passionate, intelligent; and that night when they had

made love he had been so tender, so gentle. But then afterwards, in the cold light of day, her own sense of self-revulsion and shock at *her* behaviour had warned her of the danger she had placed herself in and the folly of ever allowing such a thing to happen again. And yet here she was lying awake and aching at night, needing to be held in his arms, to reach out and touch him and be touched in turn.

Angry at her own weakness, she decided to go out into the tangled garden. They had had two days of sunshine, and now suddenly she felt the need to be outside in the fresh air. Ten minutes later, dressed in an old pair of jeans she had found at the back of her wardrobe and which she couldn't remember wearing in years, the sweatshirt which belonged to her sister, and her wellingtons, she was heading for the kitchen garden.

There was something undeniably satisfying about pulling out weeds, she decided breathlessly half an hour later; perhaps because it satisfied the basic human instinct for destruction, she reflected gloomily as she tussled with a particularly deep-rooted specimen. As far as she knew it had been years since anyone had attempted to crop neat rows of carefully maintained vegetables in these plots, and she doubted if her own enthusiasm would last long enough to do more than make a half-hearted attempt at clearing this one patch. The kitchen garden was a good size and must have once delighted the eyes of the orderly with its neat paths and rigidly segmented plots, but now some of those paths were virtually obscured by undergrowth; in the fruit section the raspberry canes were a tangle

of old and new, and here and there odd crowns of
rhubarb had produced one or two sticks of fruit.

Time passed. Emily's back began to ache, but
she refused to give in—she was determined to clear
this one plot. If nothing else, she would perhaps
grow peas in it—fresh garden peas were next to impossible to buy these days unless one knew an en-
thusiastic gardener with a surplus and no freezer.

Hard at work, concentrating her mind on her
plans for the bed once she had cleared it, refusing
to allow herself the dangerous luxury of focusing
her thoughts on Matt, she was oblivious to the
return of the two men.

The Jaguar which Matt drove had a smooth,
almost silent engine and he and John were inside
the house without Emily having heard a sound.
From his bedroom window, Matt had an excellent
view of the back garden and especially the kitchen
garden. He frowned as he saw her crouched figure,
tugging fiercely, bent over her self-imposed task.

Was it his imagination, or was there genuinely
something lonely and vulnerable about that slim,
narrow back? As he watched, she paused, pushing
back strands of hair. She had the kind of face that
suited her sleek bob, but he much preferred her hair
slightly tangled as it had been when... He found
himself swallowing hard, unable to drag his gaze
away from the small figure so far below him.

It was no use him telling himself, as he had done
night after night since his arrival here, that she was
just another Jolie, another cheat, even if this time
he was the man she was cheating with rather than
cheating against. He could not summon the fierce
protective disgust that had enabled him to turn away

from Jolie with his self-respect, if not his pride, intact.

He had tried telling himself that both Emily's shock when he had arrived here, and her determination to make it plain to him that what had happened between them was something she preferred to pretend had never taken place, showed the kind of woman she was: a woman who was prepared to cheat on the man to whom she was really supposed to be committed, a woman who did not flinch from making love with a complete stranger. And yet, no matter how many times he told himself that that was the real Emily, his heart refused to listen and repeatedly tormented him with images and memories of their shared night, of her softness and warmth, her heart-touching mixture of innocence and frankness, her almost loving desire to give him pleasure as well as take it for herself.

He supposed there was a certain macabre humour in the fact that she so obviously appeared to believe that he was the type of man who only wanted sexual contact with her. The pride in her eyes when she had told him that she was not going to make love with him again had touched something deep down inside him, and he couldn't stop himself from feeling that she was almost like two completely different people: one was the passionate, loving woman he had held in his arms and felt his body and heart respond to in a way he had grown to think impossible; the other was the shallow, cold-hearted cheat who could make love with him while she was engaged to someone else. And then there was the fact that she had been a virgin. Was *that* why she had turned to him? Had she perhaps been afraid that her fiancé might reject her for her lack of experience? It seemed a far-fetched conclusion, and surely if this man loved her, truly loved her, he would not care what degree of sexual experience she did or did not possess. For himself... but no, that way only lay pain.

Travis—what kind of name was that? He was Australian, she had said. Didn't the man realise what he was risking in leaving her on her own? Didn't he care?

Down in the garden, Emily stood up stiffly, stretched her cramped muscles. She had cleared a satisfyingly large patch of soft brown earth; now she needed to find somewhere to dispose of her large pile of weeds.

As she stretched and her aching muscles complained, she grimaced, turning to look at the house, her eyes instinctively focusing on Matt's bedroom window. The shock of seeing him standing there looking down at her robbed her of breath. She had had no idea that the two men had come back, even though she now realised that the angle of the sun ought to have warned her how long she had been outside.

Immediately she was conscious of her muddy, untidy state, of the wisps of hair clinging to her hot face, her mud-streaked jeans and the hot stickiness of her flesh.

Matt, watching her... why? Her heart was thumping too heavily; she felt dizzy... nervous. Why did she have to imagine that Matt had been watching her? He could simply have been looking out of the window. And yet she had felt, as she looked up at him, that he *had* been watching her.

Suddenly she felt exposed, vulnerable. She wanted to get inside. She wanted to shower and tidy herself up. She hurried towards the kitchen door, tugging off her wellingtons in the porch and padding inside in her socks. As she opened the door into the hall, Matt was crossing the room. Both of them froze, each watching the other.

'I didn't realise you were back,' Emily said jerkily. 'I'll just go and get changed and then I'll make some tea.'

'I can do that.'

How different he was from Uncle John; from her father, who, for all his belief in the freedom of the individual, nevertheless was quite happy to be waited on virtually hand and foot by their housekeeper.

He stood to one side so that she could walk past him, a courteous, good-mannered gesture that left her irritated with herself because of her own reluctance to get too close to him. It was ridiculous of her to imagine that he was going to reach out and grab hold of her. Why should he want to? Fiercely concentrating on the stairs, she made herself walk towards them, and then, just as she had placed her foot on the first stair, he turned round, placing his hand over hers. It was just as she remembered it to be: warm, the palm slightly callused, a man's hand, firm, and yet gentle at the same time, as though he knew how vulnerable she was and wanted to reassure her that she had nothing to fear.

She could have pulled away; she could simply have carried on and walked upstairs and away from him, but for some reason she did neither. Instead, she stayed where she was, tense and slightly breathless, watching with large apprehensive eyes as he came closer to her and then lifted his free hand to brush his thumb lightly across her cheekbone.

'Mud,' he told her laconically, and she knew from the gritty, tight feeling of her skin that he wasn't lying. She went scarlet with mortification. What a picture she must present: hair all untidy, face dirty, jeans and sweatshirt liberally flecked with the same dried mud he had just wiped off her face.

'I've been working in the garden,' she told him defensively.

'I know. I saw you. Weeding's very therapeutic, isn't it?'

How could he have possibly known of the tensions and needs which had driven her outside in the first place—or the tormenting ache that was destroying her sleep and her peace of mind?

His hand was still resting against her face, and, as though he felt the tension that ran through her, his thumb stroked soothingly across her cheekbone—a gentling, tender touch meant to impart reassurance and caring. Not a passionate touch at all, but her senses were so starved of any kind of physical contact with him that immediately her body responded to his touch like dry timber to a flame.

She knew that he must have felt her tremble, but mercifully the other and far more betraying evidence of her desire for him was hidden by the enveloping folds of her sweatshirt. *She* knew that, beneath its thick weight, her nipples had peaked and tightened, pushing eagerly against the soft cotton of her bra—but Matt, thank God, couldn't be aware of it.

It was bad enough that he had felt that sharp tremor, had monitored it with the light touch of his thumb against her cheekbone and the firm clasp of his fingers around her wrist.

He tightened that clasp now, lifting her unresisting hand from the newel post and carrying it palm upwards to his lips. The sensation of them moving softly along her skin until they rested against the frantic pulse in her wrist turned her bones to fluid.

She wanted to sink down to the floor where she stood, to simply dissolve and be absorbed by him so that she was forever a part of him—and then he said her name, releasing her from the thrall of his touch, enabling her to draw back from him and say shakily, 'I must get changed. Uncle John will be wondering where on earth I am. Peter rang this morning.'

Immediately she saw Matt's expression change, his mouth hardening, his eyes cool and watchful. 'Does he know you're engaged yet?' he asked her savagely. 'Or do you plan to wait until after you've been to bed with him before telling him?'

It was a cruel, uncalled-for remark, as Matt knew quite well, just as he knew quite well that it was the apprehension in her eyes which had sparked it. He hated the fact that she seemed to be so afraid of him. What did she think he was going to do, for heaven's sake? Force her to go to bed with him? His stomach clenched in revulsion. Didn't she *know* that that was the last thing he would do? Couldn't she tell that—that what? he asked himself bitterly as he watched her almost run upstairs. That he loved her... Impossible—how could he? She was everything he most despised in her sex. Another Jolie.

Upstairs, in the privacy of her room, Emily refused to allow herself to dwell on what Matt had said, quickly pulling clothes off hangers and hurrying into the bathroom. Once there she stripped off her filthy things and stood under the sting of the room's old-fashioned shower.

How dare Matt suggest... imply... did he really believe that she would? She bit her lip in anguish. Of course he believed it—and why not? After all, as far as he was concerned, she had had sex with him while engaged to someone else.

She had never felt so confused in all her life. Her nights were tormented by memories of tenderness and sharing so strong that she couldn't believe they were just an illusion; but then, with daybreak, and the cold, clear light of day, she was forced to acknowledge that, if their lovemaking had meant something more to Matt than merely a one-night stand, he would have made some attempt to get in touch with her, to trace her. And nothing could eradicate the damning knowledge that when they had met again it had been a cold-blooded resumption of their sexual relationship that had concerned him and not the establishment of any emotional bonding.

Tired and confused, she found herself wishing that she were a thousand miles away from Matt. And all the heartache his presence was causing her.

The truth was that if Matt actually chose to try to persuade her to go to bed with him again, she didn't think she would have the willpower to refuse. She shivered inwardly. What was happening to her? It was almost as though, somewhere on that drive back from her parents', her lifelong habits of caution and self-preservation had given way to a dangerous recklessness which, once given life, refused to be safely locked away again. Somehow or other, in meeting Matt she had exposed herself to some dangerously rebellious aspects of her own personality, aspects which had hitherto been hidden from her. Either that or she had quite simply fallen instantly and deeply in love with the man. And that, of course, was impossible. Wasn't it?

Of course it was. It must be. It *had* to be.

CHAPTER EIGHT

It was almost six weeks now since Matt had moved into the house, and every day Emily's ability to distance herself from him seemed to wear a little thinner. She had tried keeping herself as physically apart from him as she could, even going to the extent of inventing work she just had to do in the office so that she could avoid eating with the two men.

Uncle John, vague and totally wrapped up in his own affairs, barely seemed to notice whether she joined them or not. But Matt did, and seemed to take a perverse pleasure in deliberately seeking her out, in deliberately invading her solitude; always with a perfectly legitimate excuse—some papers her uncle needed, a cup of tea he had just made, a message he had to give her. And Emily had no idea how on earth she was going to get through the remainder of his six-month stay.

She had learned from snippets of conversation at the dinner table that Matt was filling in temporarily for another don before considering whether or not to take over the post on a full-time basis. Uncle John was urging him to accept, pointing out the advantages of such a post.

During one such conversation, Matt agreed quietly, 'It would be an excellent career move, and I'd be entering a very privileged world—but there are other universities, other students...'

'Not like Oxford,' Uncle John had protested, and unwillingly Emily had felt herself drawn even more to Matt. He embodied so many of the virtues she had once invented for her fictional heroes—but there was another side to him, as she had already discovered.

She had virtually forgotten about Travis's parents' impending visit to Britain until she received a letter from her sister. Reading it, she gnawed anxiously at her bottom lip, wondering how on earth she was going to maintain the fiction of being engaged to Travis himself when his parents were bound to refer to the fact that he was actually engaged to her sister.

Initially, when she had lied about being engaged to Travis, she had not thought beyond the immediate situation. Then Matt's stay with her uncle had only been intended to last for six weeks; now it had been extended for the full term of his six-month contract—something which she had had no control to veto. The house was, after all, her uncle's.

Now, reading Gracie's letter, she wondered frantically if she could possibly arrange for Travis's parents to stay somewhere else. But where? Uncle John's house was large enough to accommodate half a dozen extra guests, and was ideally situated for exploring that part of the country they were most anxious to see. Added to that was the fact that Travis's parents were almost family, and Emily's most deep-rooted instincts rebelled at the thought of being so inhospitable as to turn them away.

When she approached Uncle John to ask him if he would mind having two extra visitors, explaining evasively who they were, she was half hoping that he would refuse, thus taking the responsibility away from her; but, as she had known at heart he would, he had simply said vaguely that it was up to her. Uncle John was a natural bachelor, even though he had actually been married; he was the kind of man who much preferred to leave the running of his household in female hands and to have as little to do with it as possible. All that he required were clean clothes, good, wholesome food and somewhere quiet to work undisturbed, and there were many times when Emily wondered why on earth he kept on the large house when he would probably have been far more comfortable living in his rooms.

A by-product of her emotional and physical anguish had been the long hours she had spent outside working in the garden. On several occasions Matt had offered to help her with this work, but she had always refused, trying not to react to the brief hardening of his mouth and eyes that greeted this refusal. She couldn't ban him from using the garden, though, and the sight of him pushing the heavy and old-fashioned lawn-mower over the now tamed lawns was one that always brought an uncomfortable kick of sensation to her stomach.

She knew that they were having a particularly warm spell of weather; she knew that pushing the mower must be hard work; but surely there was really no need for him to remove his shirt completely. Surely there was no need for him to spend so much time fiddling with whatever it was that caused the mower to be so temperamental, so that whenever she chanced to go outside invariably Matt was there, bending over the innards of the machine, his dark hair flopping over his forehead, his torso tanned by his exposure to the sun, the movement of the muscles beneath the skin reminding her all too provocatively of how those same muscles had once reacted to her touch.

And worst of all was the fact that he seemed completely oblivious to the effect he was having on her and, as the days grew warmer and she longed to be outside working on that part of the garden which she had begun to think of as hers, she found that she was prevented from doing so by the knowledge that Matt would already be there, and that his presence put such a constraint on her that she found it impossible to work.

One particular Saturday morning, though, she was in luck. It was a wonderfully mild day, the sun shining, a fresh breeze blowing, and, when Emily was clearing away the breakfast, she was delighted to hear Matt saying something to her uncle about being ready to drive him to Oxford in half an hour's time.

That was one chore which Matt had taken over completely from her, and in other circumstances she would have been grateful to him for it. Now that she was no longer having to act as her uncle's chauffeur she had far more time on her hands, and she had even recently had to gently chivvy her uncle for more work to fill in her time.

She waited until she was sure the two men had left before hurrying up to her bedroom, and quickly removing her skirt and sweater. It was warm enough outside for her to wear a thin short-sleeved top along with her jeans and wellingtons.

The espaliered fruit trees along the back wall of the kitchen garden were full of blossom, although Matt had told her that he doubted they would produce much fruit. He had explained to her how once these trees would have been pruned and trained to grow along wires to produce the maximum amount of fruit in the minimum amount of space, and to make use of the warmth of the wall to ripen their crop.

He had been surprisingly knowledgeable, much more so than she was herself, and had casually explained that he had been brought up by his grandparents, both of whom had been very keen gardeners. He hadn't mentioned his parents, and it had been Uncle John who had told her absently one afternoon, while they were working, that they had been keen botanists and that they had been killed while hunting for rare plants when Matt had been a very small child.

Determined to make a success of her own small plot, Emily had assiduously studied gardening books, mulling over what crops she could reasonably hope to be successful with. The herbs she grew in pots always did well, and while she knew that Matt would probably have been able to tell her which crop she should experiment with first, some perverse streak of independence compelled her to ignore the overtures of friendship he seemed determined to make towards her and instead to hold herself aloof from him.

The man who sought her out while she was gardening, who brought her cups of tea while she was working, who refused to allow her to clean his room, who insisted on doing more than his fair share of the chores, was not the same man who had so brutally and casually proposed that they go to bed together. Far from it—he was instead everything she had hoped to find in a man. She dared not allow herself to respond to that Matt, and it was for that reason that she snubbed all his attempts to re-establish their relationship on a nonsexual footing.

Matt, unaware of what she was really feeling, misinterpreted her snubs and put them down to the fact that she was bitterly regretting what had happened between them and that she was determined to remind him at every turn that she was an engaged woman.

He told himself that he was being a fool for persisting, that he ought simply to ignore her, to pretend she didn't exist; but, when he had dropped John off at his friend's and arranged to pick him up later in the day, instead of driving on to Oxford as he had planned he found himself turning the car round and heading back to the house and Emily.

He found her digging energetically in the garden, her soft hair tousled, her skin flushed both by the sun and her exertions. He liked the way her top revealed the smooth, feminine flesh of her arms and clung to her breasts. Her jeans outlined the smallness of her waist and the womanly roundness of her bottom.

Unaware that she was being watched, Emily stopped digging, leaning on her spade as she breathed deeply and surveyed what she had done.

'Runner beans would be a good crop here.'

She froze as she heard Matt's voice making the quiet suggestion, and then turned round stiffly, frowning as she realised the picture she must present. 'I didn't realise you were coming back for lunch,' she told him curtly. 'I'd better go in. Uncle John——'

'I left your uncle with his friend. I'm picking him up later.'

Emily discovered that her heart had started thumping far too fast and that it was extraordinarily difficult for her to breathe—far more difficult than it had been ten minutes ago when she had been digging so energetically.

A fierce combination of exhilaration and fear thrilled through her, so that she seemed to be conscious of both herself and Matt on two different and separate levels. On one level her senses relayed to her the fact that she felt hot and grubby, and that she felt self-conscious about her untidy hair and flushed skin. She could see Matt looking at her, watching her, and she couldn't help contrasting his clean jeans and well-groomed appearance with her own. On the second, deeper level, though, she had a different awareness—an awareness of the fact that in merely glancing at Matt's hands she was remembering how they had felt moving against her skin; that, in briefly noting his clean jeans and soft cotton shirt, she was remembering how his body had looked without clothes, how it had felt . . .

She licked her lips nervously, shifting her weight from one foot to the other, wishing he would go away and yet, conversely, dangerously, wanting him to stay.

Desperate to banish this latter weakness she demanded angrily, 'What is it you want, Matt?'

'You know what I want,' he told her flatly. 'I want you.'

She felt the heat invade her skin, prickling along her nerve-endings; it was useless to pretend shock or outrage—hadn't she known inwardly all the time just what kind of response she was prompting?

'I'm engaged,' she reminded him, turning her head as she uttered the lie.

For a moment he was silent, and then he said curtly, 'So you are. I wonder what this fiancé of yours would think if he knew that you and I have made love, Emily.'

She felt the blood drain from her skin as the shock of his statement hit her; for a moment she felt sick, dizzy—and then from somewhere she found the strength to say huskily, 'I don't want to discuss it, Matt, and if you think you're going to blackmail me into going to bed with you——'

'Blackmail you!'

If she hadn't known better, Emily would have believed that the harsh exclamation held genuine horror, but she ignored her own wanton need to make excuses for him, to look for something in his desire for her that she already knew didn't exist, and said fiercely instead, 'Don't try to deny it. You made it clear what you wanted from me the moment you arrived here. Just because we've...made l— had sex once, that doesn't mean it's an experience I want to repeat. As a matter of fact, I didn't even particularly enjoy it,' she lied, deliberately keeping her face averted and then holding her breath. Surely that should do it. No man liked having his sexual expertise called into question.

Matt frowned as he looked at her tense body and averted face; something here wasn't ringing true. She might not want him to make love to her now, but as for not enjoying it when they had... Her throat was flushed from the sun; a pulse beat frantically at the base of it and he had to subdue a wild impulse to imprison it with his mouth and hold it imprisoned until he felt all her restraint drain away from her.

'Not as much as you enjoy sex with your fiancé,' he said instead, and then waited.

Surreptitiously Emily crossed her fingers behind her back. 'No,' she agreed curtly, 'but then of course there is a difference. I ... I love him, while you——'

'Were just a substitute because he was unavailable,' Matt finished for her. Curiously he didn't seem angry, as she had expected. In fact, he wasn't betraying any emotion at all, and that disconcerted her.

'I'm sorry you didn't enjoy it, Emily,' he added softly, 'because I certainly did.'

She turned her head, startled shock widening her eyes as she discovered how much closer to her he was.

'I enjoyed it very much indeed,' he told her, still walking towards her, coming so close to her that for a moment she was actually tempted to abandon the spade she was clutching and to run as fast and as far as she could. Only there was nowhere to run to, and Matt was still speaking, talking to her in a soft, low voice that seemed to have a mesmeric effect on her motor system, paralysing her where she stood.

'You know, these last few weeks while I've been living here in such proximity to you, I haven't been able to stop wondering what it would be like to make love to you on a wide, comfortable bed, instead of on the hard floor of a Land Rover. I haven't been able to stop wondering what it would be like to look at you as well as touch you.'

He was standing close enough now to reach out and slip his arms round her so that he could pull her right up against his body. Emily shuddered at the contact of his hands smoothing the bare skin of her arms.

'I'm sorry you didn't share my pleasure in our lovemaking,' Matt was murmuring softly against her ear, making her body shiver as darts of sensation pierced it.

'I'd like you to share that pleasure, Emily,' he was saying hypnotically as his lips moved gently against her skin and his hands slid down her back, urging her still closer to his body.

The tension inside her was like a metal band breaking her in two; one half of her yearned desperately to give in, to melt against him, to wrap her arms around him and to turn her head so that the tormenting pressure of his mouth was caressing her lips. She wanted to tug his shirt out of his jeans and slide her hands up over his back, she wanted... She wanted it all. Everything she had had before and more—and yet at the same time she wanted to push him away from her and take to her heels and run away from him. This wasn't right. Before... before she had blinded herself to reality, had allowed herself to be caught up in the mystery of the moment—but now Matt was no longer a stranger, now she knew him, now she knew what he wanted from her and what he didn't want. She couldn't make love with him now. Not knowing how little she really mattered to him as a human being.

His hand cupped her face, turning it gently, while his lips feathered lightly against hers and his tongue circled their trembling warmth.

'You taste of sunshine and fresh air,' he whispered against her mouth, and the vibration of the words sent tiny tremors of excitement pulsing through her. 'Let me taste all of you, Emily, and show you how much pleasure I can really give you.'

Her whole body trembled under the sensual onslaught of the words. His mouth hardened over hers, the pressure of his arms tightening her awareness of his body that much more intimately as she recognised his arousal and found it fuelling her own.

He was kissing her as she had dreamed of his kissing her ever since that first night, his hands tangled in her hair, his body hard and urgent against hers, his mouth compelling, demanding. Shock after shock of urgent sensation quivered through her, the slight friction of his body moving against hers as he kissed her, stimulating her body so that her breasts swelled and tightened and the memory of the exquisite sensation of his mouth tugging at their hard crests made her move eagerly and instinctively in response to that stimulation, her body adapting itself to the contours of his so willingly, so eagerly that Matt felt his self-control splinter and he wondered if she had any real idea of what she was doing to him.

When he untangled one hand from her hair and eased it between their bodies so that he could cup the soft weight of her breast, Emily made a delirious sound of pleasure under his mouth, and trembled wildly as his thumb-tip brushed erotically against her nipple over and over again until there was nothing she wanted more than to drag his head down against her breast and to feel his mouth tugging fiercely on that small aching point of flesh.

Her top was old and worn with buttons down the front that yielded easily despite the impatience Matt could feel building up inside him. Just remembering how she had felt in his mouth, how she had reacted to the intimacy of it, was driving him crazy with the need to experience it again.

Emily felt the cool, fresh air strike wantonly against her skin as Matt cupped her breast, releasing the pale, soft flesh from its prison of fabric, exposing it momentarily to the warmth of the sun and the cool sharpness of the wind so that its smoothness was briefly disturbed by a rash of goosebumps.

There was something wildly sensual about the sensation of fresh air against her bare skin, Emily recognised feverishly, her back arching in a silent supplication, her nails digging into Matt's shoulders in sudden ecstasy as she felt the heat of his mouth against her breast. The coolness of the fresh air, the warmth of Matt's mouth, the fierce sound of pleasure he made, and her own acknowledgement of the pleasure he was giving her—they were like twin rivers, running together, blending, mingling.

There was nothing she wanted more now than for Matt to make love to her—nothing. She felt his teeth against her nipple and shuddered with pleasure, raking her nails against his skin, wanting him, needing him, loving him... Loving him. Loving him! But she couldn't—must not!

He had released her breast and covered it with his hand. His mouth was caressing her throat, but, as he felt her tension, he stopped and looked at her. 'What is it? What's the matter?'

She was too distressed to lie. 'I can't do this, Matt,' she told him brokenly. 'Please don't make me.'

She was trembling so much that he frowned, instinctively pulling her closer, trying to ease whatever it was that was distressing her so much. 'Is it because of him? Your fiancé,' he guessed, watching her.

Emily looked blankly at him. What was he talking about? And then she remembered and guilty colour flooded her face. 'Yes...yes, it is,' she fibbed, and then bit her lip, honesty compelling her to add, 'It isn't just that, though. Even if I weren't engaged, I couldn't—I want you, Matt,' she told him bravely, unable to look at him now, but unable to lie either, and what was the point? Her body had well and truly given her away. 'But I can't have a relationship with someone that's just based on sex. It would never be enough... We both know that—that you can arouse me. I've tried to pretend that it isn't true. I've tried to resist this—this physical thing between us, but...but I can't do it without your help. Please, Matt, help me. If I make love

with you now, I'll lose what's left of my self-respect.
I . . .'

The intensity of the emotion that filled him
stunned Matt. He had wanted her, desired her,
hated her almost at times, but now suddenly he was
filled with such admiration for her, such compassion, that he couldn't stop himself from lifting
his hand to her face and slowly brushing his fingers
against it, trying to both comfort her and soothe
her at the same time, trying to convey without
words all that he felt for her.

'I think I understand,' he said quietly. 'Physically you want me, but you love someone else. I
never intended to pressure you into making love
with me, Emily. I just hoped——' He broke off,
knowing there was no point now in telling her what
he had hoped.

'The last thing I want is for anything that happens
between us to rob you of your self-respect.' There
was one thing he ached to ask her, but now wasn't
the right time. *Why*, when she loved this other man
so much, had they not been lovers?

She was still trembling, her eyes huge and dark,
her face fragile and pale. Automatically, Matt
started to close the buttons on her top, dressing her
gently as though she were a child.

'I'm sorry about what I said before, about not
enjoying it when you made love to me,' Emily told
him jerkily. 'I was frightened, you see . . .'

There was so much pain in her eyes that Matt
felt as though he wanted to take hold of her and
hold on to her forever. What kind of man was this
fiancé of hers? Didn't he realise what his careless
treatment of her was doing to her? She needed him

here, not in Australia. And it didn't help that he himself was still aching with the desire that just being with her seemed to arouse.

Desire . . . he smiled grimly to himself. When was he going to admit that what he felt was far more than that? He had told himself after Jolie that he would never make the mistake of falling in love again, that he would never expose himself to that kind of pain, that kind of anguish a second time, but emotionally then he had been little more than a child. What he had felt for Jolie had been infatuation; when she had rejected him his pride had been bruised and that bruising had been painful, but what he felt for Emily went way, way beyond the mild infatuation he had felt for Jolie.

He ought to have realised what was happening to him weeks ago—his anger and disappointment when all his enquiries had failed to reveal any trace of her. Now he knew why. He had been looking for a Francine when he ought to have been searching for an Emily. Neither had it occurred to him that Emily would have had her car transported down to Oxford for it to be repaired. No wonder they had never heard of her in any of the garages he had tried. But now he had found her, and much good it was doing him.

She loved someone else. It had been easier for him when he had believed she was another Jolie, cheating on someone she professed to love without guilt or compunction. Now he knew better. There had been no mistaking the genuine confusion and shock in her voice when she had told him she wanted him and what that wanting was doing to her. He had never expected such honesty. It had taken his breath away, compelled him to listen, made him ache to comfort her, to hold and protect her.

She wanted him, but she loved someone else. As he watched her walk unsteadily away from him, he kicked savagely at the plastic bucket she had left on the pathway, wishing he could tear down the barriers between them, wishing he could tell her that what they had shared was rare and special, and that two people who reacted to one another as they did could never remotely describe what they had shared as merely sex; but to do that would mean revealing that he knew that she and this Travis had never made love, and he knew instinctively that she would hate him for revealing that knowledge. If she couldn't bring herself to admit to him that he was her first lover, then there was no way he could force that knowledge on her.

Logically controlled human beings did not fall desperately in love between the space of one heartbeat and the next, and they certainly did not go on to consummate that love without any of the preliminaries that normally preceded such intimacy—without caution, or thought for the consequences of such lovemaking, compelled to reach out to one another by a force so strong that neither of them could resist it. Such things simply did not happen... Only they had, and he was still reeling from the shock of it; still half fighting against the implications of it. Still, until today, mentally rejecting what in his heart he knew to be the truth. That he loved Emily and that he would have loved her no matter how many fiancés she had in her life, no matter how much she herself could not or would not allow herself to recognise that love.

He could understand her feelings. She was already committed to someone else; it would be easier for her to believe herself to be motivated by physical desire than to allow the possibility that she might love him. And he was beginning to be convinced that she could love him, and that, if it weren't for this Travis, he would far more easily be able to convince her that, unorthodox though the start of their relationship had been, that did not mean that their feelings weren't real...and enduring.

In her bedroom, Emily stared unseeingly at the wall. She was still trembling from head to foot. Still trying to come to terms with the shock of discovering how much she loved Matt.

Not merely needed him, wanted him, desired him, even though she did feel all those things—she loved him as well. He had been so gentle, so understanding, so generous and caring, it was as though her perception of him had suddenly been wiped clean of most of the misconceptions and fears she had deliberately fostered within herself, and she had seen him clearly and properly for the first time—and in doing so had recognised truly for the first time what manner of man he was.

It was a very lowering sensation indeed to realise that her body, her senses, were far better judges of character than her brain, that they were far better attuned to her real needs and feelings than her conscious mind, that they had recognised within Matt, a stranger, something for which they yearned, some essential sweetness of nature, some basic generosity of heart and mind that they had reached out for. If she hadn't lied, if she had been honest with him right from the start, if . . .

But what was the use? He didn't love her. He felt sorry for her, she suspected; he desired her; but love . . . That was something else, and she would be an even greater fool than she already was if she started dreaming impossible daydreams, if she allowed herself to build a fantasy world around Matt, a world peopled by the two of them and by love— a world she knew quite well could never exist outside her imagination. A world it would be very, very dangerous to walk into, even if only in the privacy of her own thoughts.

CHAPTER NINE

Now, after wishing for so long that the lengthy months of Matt's stay would pass as quickly as days, Emily found herself clinging desperately to the time that was left. She didn't want him to go, and yet in so many ways she couldn't bear him to stay. Every time he looked at her, every time he so much as walked into the same room, she was so intensely aware of him that her body seemed to be in a constant state of intense tension.

When he touched her by accident, while he was helping her with the household chores, his touch was both purgatory and heaven. She was so desperately afraid of betraying what she felt that she found herself going to extraordinary lengths just to avoid being with him.

She had lost weight, her face and body gaining a haunting fragility that made Matt frown and mentally curse this fiancé who could leave her like this, when she was so plainly pining for him. It made his heart ache to see her drawn, wan face, and sometimes it was almost impossible for him to stop himself from reaching out to her and taking her in his arms. Instead, he spent his spare time working in the garden, trying to dissipate the emotional trauma he was suffering in hard physical work.

Three months after Matt had moved in with them, Emily set out for Oxford to do her monthly domestic shop. Matt had offered to go with her, but she had refused his offer. Things were bad enough as it was. Odd how a simple and very mundane chore such as supermarket shopping could become fraught with emotional anguish and delight when that chore was performed with Matt.

Matt watched her drive away wishing there were something he could do to ease her obvious distress... wishing there were some magic formula he could use to make her stop loving this Travis and love him instead.

It seemed so unfair: she liked him, she desired him physically—but she loved someone else, and, no matter how much he lay in bed at night aching for her, he couldn't use the physical desire she felt for him to draw her into his arms. Not when she had begged him not to, when she had let down her defences and pleaded with him not to let her break the commitment she had made to someone else.

In other circumstances, he would have been pleased with the work he had done in the garden; his thorough weeding of the tangled herbaceous border had revealed several large clumps of peonies, complete with fat, bursting pink buds, and, next to them, the feathery fronds of pale pink poppies. Along the wall were old-fashioned climbing roses and clinging to them clematis, while in the middle of the wall grew a stately and very old wistaria, with a gnarled trunk, and the most stubbornly rooted couch grass he had ever come across in his life growing happily at its base.

He was tackling this determined and obstinate intruder when he heard a car. At first he thought it was John returning early from a visit to a friend, but when he went to investigate it wasn't John clambering stiffly and slowly from the interior of the stationary car but a tall, energetic-looking blonde with a mane of tousled hair and a wide, friendly smile.

'Hi, I'm Gracie,' she introduced herself, coming towards him and adding quizzically, 'Emily's sister.' And then she turned back towards the car, and held out her hand to the even taller, blonder man who was unfolding himself from the driver's seat. 'And this is my fiancé, Travis.'

She wasn't looking directly at Matt as she made this announcement, for which he was acutely grateful. He heard her saying something about only having arrived back in England the previous evening and deciding to surprise Emily with a visit on their way north.

'Where is she, by the way?' she asked him, turning back to look at him.

'Er... out shopping.' He knew he was speaking jerkily, nervously almost, and that he couldn't keep his eyes off the man standing at her side. The friendliness of Gracie's initial greeting was now held in check, a cool scrutiny taking its place.

'You are the Matt Slater whom Emily told us was staying here, aren't you?' Gracie interrogated him sharply.

Numbly Matt nodded his head, and then, with none of his usual finesse or care, he blurted out, 'Your engagement—how long...when did you...?'

Out of the corner of his eye he saw Travis move forward, frowning. Gracie squeezed her fiancé's hand and said evenly, 'We got engaged at Christmas. We met while I was out in Australia.'

It was Matt's turn to frown now. What on earth was going on? 'Was Emily with you in Australia?' he asked, wondering if it might have been that Emily had flown out to visit her sister.

'Emily, in Australia?' Gracie gave a rich chuckle. 'Good heavens, no. Emily hates travelling. She always has done; she says it's because she and I saw so little of our folks while we were growing up because they were away so much. It's as much as she can be persuaded to do to drive north to see Mum and Dad. No, Emily likes to put her roots down firmly and deeply in one place. When will she be back, by the way?'

'Back?' Matt focused on them with difficulty. Travis was still frowning at him, and he could sense that the other man didn't like the way he had been questioning Gracie. There was so much here that just didn't make sense. So much that was muddled and confused. He could spend all day carefully and discreetly trying to fish for information, but he sensed that this huge, frowning Australian would object quite forcefully to any more questions about their engagement, unless Matt furnished them with an explanation for his curiosity. Much as he hated the idea of discussing his private feelings, his private life and that of Emily with someone else, there was too much at stake for him to risk losing Emily simply because he had not wanted to reveal what he was feeling to a third party.

Looking directly at both of them he said quietly, 'Listen, I know this may sound odd, but I need to talk to both of you—and before Emily comes back.' He saw the look of concern that darkened Gracie's eyes and the way Travis's hand closed protectively around hers, and reassured her quickly, 'No, nothing's wrong. Emily is fine. It's just that... Why don't we go inside? I'll make some tea and we can talk.'

Half an hour later, Gracie was staring at him in open amusement.

'Emily pretended that she was engaged to Travis? But why? What on earth did you do to her?'

'I made love to her,' Matt admitted shortly, and suddenly Gracie wasn't looking amused any longer. Neither was Travis. Gracie stood up. She was a tall woman, much taller than Emily, but still a good few inches short of Matt's height. Even so, there was something quite definitely intimidating about the way she paced the floor—a lioness, all too ready and willing to protect her defenceless young. 'You did what?' she demanded ominously.

'I made love to her,' Matt repeated firmly, and then added just as firmly, 'She *is* a woman, you know, and not a child.'

'She's also my sister,' Gracie told him flatly. 'She's led a very sheltered and protected life. There was a man while she was at university... She had virtually chosen her wedding dress when she found out that he'd simply been using her.'

She was giving him a hard stare. 'Emily might be my older sister, but she's very vulnerable... very timid about the way she lives her life. I can't think of any reason why she'd allow you to make love to her and then tell you she was engaged to someone else, unless she had found the experience so unpleasant that there was no way she wanted to repeat it.'

'Or unless she found it completely the opposite,' Travis intervened quietly.

Matt looked at him gratefully. 'I think she loves me, and I certainly love her,' he told them both, openly admitting his feelings, 'but there've been so many misunderstandings and misconceptions between us...' He spread his hands in mute explanation of the complexity of the situation.

'If I went to Emily and told her that I know this engagement of hers is a fiction, if I told her how I feel about her, I doubt that she'd believe me. I don't think she has the self-confidence to trust either what she feels, or me. I need to get closer to her, to win her trust, and I think I know the way.'

While he talked, Gracie and Travis listened. Once or twice, Gracie interrupted him, questioning him sharply, but slowly her hostility evaporated and amusement took its place. 'I'm not sure that I should be agreeing to this,' she told him, once they had both promised to help him. 'And if you hadn't assured me that Emily won't be hurt——'

'If she hadn't lied to me, none of this would be necessary,' Matt pointed out with a certain amount of grimness. While he thought he could understand what had motivated her, when he thought of all the unhappiness she had caused them both by her creation of her fictitious fiancé, he wasn't sure if it wouldn't do her good to suffer a little.

When he carried the tea-tray out to the kitchen, Gracie went with him, stopping him in the hall to ask quietly, 'You do love her, don't you, Matt?'

'Yes,' he told her simply. 'Otherwise I wouldn't be doing any of this.'

* * *

Oxford was busy, the supermarket was hot and crowded, Emily had managed to pick the wrong queue, and then on her way to the car her trolley had almost turned over on her, and, by the time she eventually turned into the drive of Uncle John's house, she was feeling very out of sorts indeed.

She frowned a little when she saw the unfamiliar car parked in the drive, but thought little of it until she walked into the kitchen struggling with the weight of the heaviest of the cartons of groceries, which she had picked up deliberately to add to her feelings of being badly done to—and discovered her sister, Travis and Matt all busily involved in washing up, all laughing away together as though they were the best of friends, all so obviously amused by the sight of her struggling with the too-heavy box that for a moment she had a petulant impulse to hurl the thing at them and then burst into tears.

When the three of them rushed forward towards her at once, all obviously bent on relieving her of its weight, she felt like a pygmy being swooped on by a race of giants, and instead of being grateful for their assistance she said fiercely, 'It's all right, I can manage,' adding peevishly, 'After all, I *have* carried it all the way from the car.'

She saw Gracie's eyebrows lift and felt her face colour guiltily. There was no reason for her to take her bad temper out on anyone else.

'You should have come in and got Matt to carry those for you,' Gracie was saying chidingly. 'Heavens, what on earth is the point in having a fiancé if you aren't going to let him do some fetching and carrying. I promise you, I make Travis work hard—don't I, darling?'

This time Emily let go of the box, barely aware of the quick way Matt retrieved it, as she stood and stared at her sister. What on earth was Gracie talking about? And what was she doing here, anyway, and with Travis... Travis... Oh, my God.

As the realisation of her position dawned, her eyes widened, her face going white, so that Matt, who had dumped the heavy box on the table and turned round just in time to see her shock, had to quell an impulse to go over to her and take her in his arms, reminding himself sternly that what he was intending to do was in the best interests of them both. She had been evading him for so long that he suspected she would simply never accept that he loved her and had done from the first moment he had touched her.

Summoning a casual smile, he walked over to her and put his arm round her, quelling his compassion as he felt the shocked rigidity of her slender body. 'I'm afraid I've already broken our good news to your sister, darling. I didn't think you'd mind in the circumstances,' he added meaningfully, looking from her to Travis, while Emily stared at him in bewildered confusion. What on earth was going on? *Why* had Matt told Gracie that they were engaged? He must surely have realised by now that she had lied to him about Travis.

Hard on the heels of the shock of discovering Gracie's presence in the kitchen had come the appalling realisation that Matt must now know the truth: that she *wasn't* engaged to Travis and that she never had been engaged to him. She had waited, frozen, to see the look of disgust and contempt in his eyes, but instead he was gazing down at her with warmth and affection. She blinked hard as his face suddenly became distorted, and she realised that she was about to burst into tears.

'Poor darling,' she heard Matt saying softly. 'I should never have let you go to Oxford on your own. You must be exhausted. Come and sit down and I'll make you a cup of tea.'

Emily had a crazy desire to burst into peal after peal of hysterical laughter. Since when had a grown woman of twenty-six been too fragile and delicate to be allowed to do her own domestic shopping? If she was feeling weak and fragile, it had nothing to do with the bad temper and irritation which had followed her monthly trudge along the soulless aisles of the supermarket, but the discovery that her sister and Travis were here in England, in Oxfordshire—in Uncle John's house.

Somehow or other she found herself being shepherded towards the table and pushed gently, but oh, so firmly, down into a chair. She tried to stand up, but for some reason Travis and Gracie had materialised at her side, standing beside her like a pair of gaolers, she decided ungratefully.

'I don't want any tea,' she started to say. It was true; she, a virtual teetotaller, wanted nothing more than a good stiff drink—no, two good stiff drinks, she decided muzzily. What on earth was going on? If she closed her eyes and then opened them again, would everything have returned to normal?

She heard Gracie saying something about how wonderful it was that she was engaged, and that perhaps they could make it a double wedding.

Emily shuddered and actually discovered that she was looking at her left hand in bewilderment, as though half expecting to see an engagement ring materialising there. She had never particularly liked Lewis Carroll's Alice, but for the first time she actually found herself sympathising with her.

'No,' she croaked protestingly. 'Not a double wedding.' She had a momentary vision of the absurdity of it, of herself and Gracie walking down the aisle together—well, at least Gracie walking, while she almost ran to match her longer strides.

Somewhere in the distance Matt was saying lightly, 'I agree with Emily. Besides, you haven't set a date for your wedding yet, have you, while Emily and I hope to be married in June?'

In June...Emily couldn't believe what she was hearing. June was just two weeks away.

'June...But the parents aren't due back from Brazil until then,' Gracie was saying.

Emily struggled to comprehend what on earth was going on. Someone—Travis, she thought—handed her a mug of tea, which she gulped thirstily. Gracie was still talking about weddings, and Matt was saying something completely ridiculous and insane about not being prepared to wait very long to make her his wife, and that, as she had a romantic desire to marry in June, that meant that marry in June they would, whether it was only two weeks hence or not.

'Which reminds me, darling,' Matt added, coming towards her, and somehow or other elbowing Travis out of the way so that he was standing right beside her, his arm draped very possessively along her shoulders. 'Did you finally decide on a dress?' He turned to Gracie, and to Emily's stunned horror told her confidingly, 'She's refusing to wear white, silly thing. After all, in this day and age, and feeling as we do about one another...'

The look he gave her would have burned holes in metal, Emily decided disbelievingly. It was certainly doing the most incomprehensible things to her insides... almost making her believe that that burning, melting look of desire was actually real, and not simply fabricated for heaven alone knew what purpose.

'But she tells me she's found something she likes in cream. Personally, I'd like to see her in something very twenties-style, all soft, flowing satin or chiffon and heavy antique lace——'

'Oh, yes, that would be just right for you,' Gracie chimed in. 'If you haven't found anything yet, there's a place in London that specialises in the most wonderful period clothes.'

Emily discovered that her hands had curled into protesting fists and that, moreover, she wanted very badly indeed to open her pretty mouth and scream loudly. Her head was buzzing and aching, she felt as though she had strayed into a scene from a play where everyone apart from her knew their lines, she couldn't understand why Matt wasn't demanding to know why she had lied about being engaged to Travis, and, most of all, she could not understand how she had supposedly come to be engaged to him.

Engaged to him. The shudder that racked her body was so self-illuminating that Matt who was watching her had to fight not to take hold of her and make love to her so passionately, so lovingly, that she wouldn't be able to resist loving him in turn.

Loving him. Was he deluding himself in believing that she did love him, that this whole ridiculous situation had arisen because neither of them had had the courage to tell each other when they had made love just what they had really been feeling, because neither of them had had the breadth of imagination, the trust, to accept the precious gift they had been given?

'Emily, we were hoping you could put us up here for a few days,' Gracie was saying. 'We want to have a good look round so that when Travis's parents arrive we can make sure they see everything they ought to see. Matt said he didn't think there'd be any problem with us staying.' She pulled a face and added drily, 'I suppose for Uncle John's sake we'd better follow your example and have separate rooms, but next to one another, please. You and Matt might not mind flitting up and down the landing...'

She ignored the gasp Emily gave, just as Matt ignored the rigid tension in her shoulders.

'Come on. Show me which rooms we can have,' Gracie pressed. 'And you can tell me more about what's been going on, as well,' she added cheerfully. 'Fancy not letting me know you were engaged.'

'It was very sudden,' Matt said breezily.

Emily found she was trembling when she stood up. Somehow or other Matt was standing right in front of her, and as she tried to step past him he moved as well, so that she walked straight into him.

He put his arms out, to steady her she supposed, but what actually happened was that they closed round her, and the warm, familiar, arousing man-smell of him went straight to her head like wine and she had a dizzying impulse to simply lean against him and howl like a child.

Indeed, she discovered that she actually *was* leaning against him, and that one of his hands was cradling the back of her neck, burrowing beneath her hair to stroke the tension from the overstrained muscles there.

She felt his breath against her hair and then her ear as he bent his head to murmur, 'Don't be long, will you. I want to show you what I've been doing in the garden.'

As she lifted her head she saw Gracie's amusement, and felt herself flushing.

'Emily and I share an interest in gardening,' Matt told her sister loftily. 'We've both been working very hard to try and resuscitate the garden here. In fact, we've both fallen in love with it so much that we're hoping your Uncle John will sell the place to us.'

If anyone other than herself was conscious of her shock, they didn't betray it. What on earth was Matt saying? Just for one heart-stopping second she had felt her heart leap fiercely with joy and excitement and had known illuminatingly just how much she would have loved to make her home here, and then she had fallen swiftly and painfully into the pit of truth, and had known how stupid she was being. She had no idea what was going on, but the moment she and Matt were alone she intended to find out.

But first she had to take Gracie upstairs and show her the spare rooms. Fiercely hot colour dyed her skin as she pulled away from Matt and heard him whisper, loud enough for Gracie and Travis to hear, 'The sooner you and I are married, the better. Gracie is quite right, I'm tired of having to leave you on your own and go back to my own bed.'

Emily didn't know where to look. Why on earth was Matt making such outrageous remarks? He must know... What? That her sister, who knew her so well, would never believe she would have such an intimate relationship with someone unless she was deeply, wildly in love with them and knew that that love was returned in equal measure.

It was all very well for him to talk about a marriage between them as though it were an accepted fact, and certainly he was lying very convincingly—even she, for one light-headed moment, had almost believed...but sooner or later Gracie would have to know the truth.

As she turned towards the door, Matt pulled her briefly to him so that her back was to the others, and then, as he bent his head down to her, pressing his mouth first against her temple, so that she shivered involuntarily, **and** then lingeringly and devastatingly against her mouth, so that she swayed and fought dizzily against an overwhelming impulse to fling her arms around him and hold on to him, he whispered against her lips, 'Meet me in the garden as soon as you can, and I'll explain.'

So there *was* an explanation. She had no idea what on earth it could be, she reflected numbly as she led Gracie upstairs. Needless to say, as soon as they were out of earshot of the two men, Gracie rounded on her and took hold of her shoulders, saying teasingly, 'What a dark horse you are, Emmy... All those letters and never once any hint of what was going on. Oh, you mentioned Matt right enough, but if I hadn't read between the lines I'd have had no idea.'

Read between the lines. Emily's face flamed as she wondered what on earth she must have betrayed so unknowingly, unaware that her sister was using a little licence of her own in maintaining Matt's fiction.

However, the sight of Emily's pale, drawn face caused Gracie to have a small pang of compunction. Emily had already suffered once by loving a man. She paused halfway up the stairs and stood there, making Emily feel even more like a dwarf as she stood looking back up at her.

'I like him, darling, and it's plain he adores you,' Gracie told her, 'but you've hardly said a word, and you look so tense. You do love him, don't you?'

Here was her chance to say that she had no idea what was going on, and that she and Matt were most definitely not engaged. Here was her chance, so why on earth wasn't she seizing hold of it? Why on earth was she saying shakily, and oh so truthfully, to her sister, 'Yes. Yes, I do love him.'?

And with such conviction in her voice that Gracie smiled happily back at her, and said cheerfully, 'Well, that's all right then. Now, show me these rooms Travis and I are to have. Poor Travis,' she added with a chuckle. 'He won't take kindly to our having separate rooms. Your Matt must have the self-restraint of a saint. I'm not surprised he's not willing to have a long engagement. You'll have a church wedding, of course, and at home. Look, Travis and I are on our way up there—why don't I have a word with the vicar and fix things up with him while I'm there? Matt told us that you were both hoping to take a couple of days off to make all the arrangements, but that you were reluctant to leave Uncle John. We could easily——'

Emily managed a strangled, 'No,' which caused Gracie to stop and turn to look at her. 'I...I haven't written and told Mum and Dad yet,' Emily told her weakly.

Gracie seemed to accept her explanation, although she did warn, 'Well, you're cutting it a bit fine, you know. I appreciate that Matt doesn't have any family and that you'll only be having a small reception, and that you want it at home, but there'll still be an awful lot of organising to be done, and if you think that Louise is going to let you off without the full works food-wise, then you don't know her as well as you ought.'

Feeling more guilty and miserable with every word her sister uttered, Emily increased her speed, hurrying her down the landing and almost pushing her into one of the spare bedrooms. 'This one has a connecting door to the one next to it,' she told her hurriedly. 'Travis——'

'They'll be ideal,' Gracie interrupted her. 'But why on earth aren't you and Matt using them? Honestly...'

She saw the way Emily flushed, and added teasingly, 'When Matt let it slip that the two of you were already lovers, I was so surprised I almost fell off my chair.'

Instead of feeling pleased, Emily was suddenly for no reason at all quite definitely angry. 'Why?' she demanded bitterly. 'Did you think I was so abnormal that I wouldn't *want* to make love with the man I love? What were we supposed to do?' she challenged. 'Wait until we're married? As you're doing?'

'Ouch. Come on, I'm not criticising,' Gracie told her gently. 'I'm all for it, and no, I don't think you're abnormal. It's just that, knowing how much Gerry hurt you...well, I'd always assumed for some reason that you'd decided to turn your back on passion and romance. Don't be cross with me, Emmy,' she coaxed. 'I didn't mean to offend you. It's only that you've always been just that little bit...'

'Prissy,' Emily suggested shortly.

'No—not prissy. I can't explain it properly. It's just that anyone who knows you couldn't help knowing that you'd never go to bed with a man unless you loved him and were in a committed relationship with him.'

Emily opened her mouth to tell her just how wrong she was, but Gracie was still speaking. 'I've always rather envied you that moral strength of mind of yours, and Matt obviously adores you. Come on, we'd better get back downstairs. I want Travis to bring up our stuff. I'm not sure how long we'll be staying yet; a few days at least. Oh, and by the way, if Uncle John should come back within the next hour, will you be a darling and tell him that Travis and I are resting—er—recovering from our jet lag,' Gracie told her, giving her a naughty grin.

When they went back downstairs, Travis had already unloaded the hired car. Matt, he explained, had gone into the garden; and, watching her sister and brother-in-law-to-be heading for the stairs, Emily knew she couldn't put it off any longer. She *had* to confront Matt and find out exactly what was going on.

CHAPTER TEN

EMILY found Matt studying the fat buds of the peonies. He didn't look up as she approached, but he must have heard her because he said enthusiastically, 'Just look at this. I'd never have believed it could survive, almost smothered by those weeds. It's going to give us a glorious show of colour——'

Emily couldn't stand it any longer. 'Matt, what's going on?' she interrupted him abruptly. '*Why* does Gracie think we're engaged?'

Matt stood up too. He was standing far too close to her—far, far too close, and when his arms suddenly closed round her and his hands ran possessively down her back, urging her so intimately close to his own body that the breath left her lungs in a single stunned gasp, she automatically tried to ease herself away from him. But Matt wouldn't let her go. Instead he brushed his lips against her ear and told her softly, 'Your sister is watching us.'

And then, as she instinctively tried to turn her head to look back at the house, Matt's hand came up to turn it back again and hold it still while his mouth moved hotly over her skin, searching almost desperately for her mouth. When he found it, he didn't kiss her gently as he had done before, nor lightly in the manner she had been expecting, but with such a depth of thrilling need that she succumbed to it immediately, her arms locking round him, her body melting into his as it had been aching to do for weeks, her lips parting sweetly and invitingly, clinging to the firm outline of his, while all the time his hands moved eagerly over her body making every part of her aware of how much his touch aroused her.

The kiss seemed to go on for ever; each time she managed to find the strength to break free of him, his mouth would caress some other part of her throat or face and, having sensitised that area to the point where her self-control had shattered, would move back to her lips as though magnetised by them, and each time he kissed her she sank deeper and deeper into the whirlpool of delight he was spinning around her.

She felt him lift her off her feet while he was still kissing her, but it wasn't until she felt his mouth trail down her throat to the exposed curve of her breast that she realised he had unfastened her blouse.

She tried to protest, to demand that he release her, to summon all the cogent and vital reasons why she should make him stop what he was doing immediately—but another and stronger feeling ran counter to this sensible plan, and the closer his seeking lips got to the hard pinnacle of her breast, the more difficult it became to hold on to her common sense. In fact, she even found herself arching eagerly towards him, wanting to assist him, wanting to feel again the sweetly agonising sensation of his mouth caressing her so intimately.

When he stopped suddenly centimetres short of his goal, and unsteadily lowered her to the ground, tugging the sides of her blouse together as he did so, she could almost have screamed with frustration.

'It's all right. They've gone now,' she heard him saying, but it was several seconds before his meaning penetrated. When it did, she went bright red and wrenched herself away from him, her fingers trembling as she fought to fasten the buttons.

'I demand to know what's going on,' she told him fiercely, conscious that her voice was shaking almost as much as her hands.

There was an odd silence, and when she automatically looked up she saw that Matt looked as flushed as she felt. 'I should have thought it was obvious,' he told her tersely. 'I wanted to make love to you.'

For a moment she stood there and let the sweet, wild tide of joy carry her, and then she dammed it and said severely, 'That wasn't what I meant. Why did you tell Gracie we were engaged?'

'What? Oh, that. Well, it seemed the best thing to do. I did it for your sake, you know,' he added in a softer voice.

'For my sake.' She was dumbfounded.

'Well, I guessed immediately what must have happened when she walked in and announced that Travis—*your* Travis—was *her* fiancé,' Matt told her quietly. 'I suppose they came here to tell you that they'd fallen for one another, and to ask you to release Travis from your engagement to him. I must say I thought it a bit thick that Gracie should actually introduce him as *her* fiancé. Perhaps I shouldn't have leapt in the way I did, but all I could think about was how you were going to feel when you came back and discovered that he'd dumped you for her.'

Matt had taken hold of her hand and was caressing it gently, and yet so arousingly that she could barely concentrate on what he was saying. Her senses were screaming out to her that they needed far more than the deliberately provocative stimulation they were getting—that they wanted his hands on her body... his mouth... his body... With an effort she tore herself from such erotic yearnings and tried to listen to what he was saying to her.

'So I thought I'd steal a march on them, so to speak, and tell them that you and I were engaged. Of course, I didn't let on that I knew that you and he...'

Matt paused and Emily stared speechlessly at him. This was the last thing she had thought of— that *Matt* should want to protect *her*, to help her. Her throat was thick with emotional tears; she longed to fling herself into his arms and howl—and even more she longed to be able to tell him the truth.

'I must say you've taken it marvellously well. I half dreaded you coming in and flinging yourself into his arms before I could say a word. You must feel like hell. And after you've struggled so hard to be faithful to your engagement,' he added innocently.

Emily still couldn't say a word.

'Of course, you won't think so now,' Matt comforted her. 'But in the long run it's probably for the best. Just imagine if he'd left you for her, after the wedding.'

The wedding. Emily suddenly remembered something far more important than her supposed broken heart over Travis. 'What on earth possessed you to tell Gracie we were getting married in June?' she demanded bitterly.

Matt looked hurt and embarrassed. 'Well, she managed to drag out of me the fact that we'd been lovers—don't ask me how—and, well, to be quite honest, after that I didn't have much option. I suppose Travis must have told her that you and he had never made love,' he added carelessly, so carelessly that for a moment Emily almost didn't take in the significance of what he was saying.

'Travis and I——

'Well, you didn't, did you?' Matt asked reasonably. 'I thought at first it must be because you were frightened he might find you inexperienced and that was why... but then when I saw him with Gracie and I learned that all three of you had been together in January, I realised that he must have been having second thoughts about your engagement then and that that was why he held back.'

Emily felt as though she'd been turned to stone. She dared not—she simply must not ask Matt how he knew that she and Travis had not been lovers. She didn't think she could bear to hear the answer.

'I... I think I'll go inside,' she said carefully instead. 'It's been a very odd sort of day.' She put her hand to her head, and wondered if she was actually awake or merely—please God—having a nightmare.

'Yes, it's not every day you lose one fiancé and gain another,' Matt said cheerfully, apparently oblivious to what she was feeling.

If he weren't still justifiably very, very angry with her, there would have been no way he could have stopped himself from taking her into his arms and confessing how much he loved her, Matt acknowledged, watching her. It was one thing to tell himself that he was doing this for both their sakes, and that, if they were to have any chance of happiness together, she must accept as he had done that there was nothing shameful or wrong in their love-making, and that, while intellectually neither of them might be able to understand it, they had actually fallen in love at first sight; it was quite another to stand here and see the misery and pain darken her eyes.

Steeling himself against that misery, Matt added, mock offendedly, 'I thought you'd be pleased. I know how you feel about your self-respect. I knew how you'd feel walking in to discover that the man you love has broken his engagement to you and become engaged to your sister. You see, the same thing once happened to me.'

He had her attention now. Her shocked gaze had fastened on his face, so he added almost carelessly, 'Of course, it was a long time ago. I was a young fool. I believed that Jolie—that was her name— loved me. In fact, what she loved was the trust fund my parents had left me. It took the discovery of her in bed with someone else to make me recognise the truth,' he added grimly. 'I know all too well what the humiliation of losing someone you love is like, Emily. I'm sorry if I've done the wrong thing. I only wanted to help.'

Emily didn't know which hurt the most: the knowledge that he had loved and probably still did love someone else; or the awareness of just how special a man he actually was to have thought of her and acted so promptly to save her from being hurt.

What he didn't know was that he had far more power to hurt her than poor Travis was ever likely to have, and in 'helping' her he had actually caused her the most appalling problems. How on earth was she going to explain away to Gracie the abrupt ending of their engagement, especially now that Gracie knew that they had been lovers and knew by her own admission that she loved him? Her head was aching with the effort of trying to come to terms with shock after shock and all in the space of one short afternoon.

'Look, it's not the end of the world,' Matt told her easily. 'Engagements are always being broken.'

'Not within two weeks of the wedding, and when the two people are supposed to be so madly in love with one another that they can't keep their hands off one another,' Emily snapped at him crossly. 'And not when one of those two people is me. Gracie knows that I... She's probably on the phone to Brazil right now telling Mum and Dad. Do you know, she actually wanted to book the church for us when she and Travis go home.'

Matt was still holding her hand, stroking his thumb over her racing pulse, but now he stopped and frowned at her, saying gently, 'But Emily, I meant your engagement to Travis.'

Emily stared at him, her skin flooding with betraying colour. She was so caught up in the trauma of somehow or other convincing Gracie that she didn't love Matt after all, that she had completely forgotten her bogus engagement to Travis.

Suddenly it was all too much for her, and, despite the fact that she was twenty-six years old, a mature woman who never gave way to her emotions but kept them locked up very firmly, she stamped her foot and said pettishly, 'Never mind my engagement to Travis. How on earth am I going to explain to Gracie that *you* and I aren't getting married?'

If he hadn't seen the shimmer of tears in her eyes, Matt might almost have burst out laughing. His self-controlled, stubborn, darling Emily was suddenly showing him very clearly just what he had to look forward to when she and he produced a daughter.

'Don't worry about it,' he comforted her. 'We'll think of something. Oh, and by the way, while you were upstairs your uncle rang. He's staying overnight with his friend and so he won't be back until tomorrow.'

In actual fact he had been the one to make the telephone call, explaining that Gracie and Travis had arrived, and playing on the older man's dislike of too much exuberant, youthful company. He was surprising himself with his talent for deceit, he decided guiltily, drawing Emily's attention to the budding peonies with an air of tranquillity that made her want to throw something at him. It was all very well for him. It wasn't his sister who believed they were passionately in love and on the verge of getting married.

As far as Emily was concerned, the rest of the day and the evening that followed it were simply a continuation of the nightmare which had begun when she had walked into the kitchen and discovered that she was engaged to Matt.

At nine o'clock, unable to stand it a moment longer, she announced with perfect truth that she had a headache and intended to go to bed. When Matt solicitously went upstairs with her, she snapped at him like a cornered cat, slamming her bedroom door in his face with a noise which did nothing to ease her pounding head.

All evening he had been attentive and lover-like, so that her nerves were stretched to breaking point with the effort of controlling her own responsiveness to him. Even now, outside her door, if he had taken hold of her and kissed her as he had done in the garden earlier, she knew she would have betrayed to him exactly how she felt about him.

She didn't know how much more she could endure; it had been one thing to control her love for him when she could maintain a physical distance between them, but now, with him so determined to play the amorous and adoring fiancé, he seemed to touch her at every opportunity, and more—he seemed to actively create such opportunities when they had no right to exist.

Her skin actually felt hot and tender with a feverish craving for the intimacy of his touch. Her body ached with tension and desire—even her brain was clouded with emotion and need. She fumbled in her handbag for some headache tablets and took two before going to bed. Somehow tomorrow she must find a way to persuade Gracie to cut short her visit. Either that or she would have to tell her the truth.

She sat bolt upright in bed and winced as her head pounded. Of course—that was what she should have done right from the start. She gnawed at her bottom lip. First thing in the morning she would explain everything to Gracie and then she would ask her, as her sister, to keep what she had told her to herself, and leave, and then once she and Travis had gone...well, then she could tell Matt that she was grateful to him but that there was no need for him to pretend to be her fiancé any longer, and that she intended to write to Gracie and tell her that their engagement was off.

Breathing a sigh of relief, she settled back in her bed and closed her eyes. Yes...that was what she would do. First thing in the morning.

Only when she woke up, it wasn't morning. It was still night and her bedroom door was open and Matt was standing inside it, whispering urgently, 'Emily, what's wrong?'

'Wrong?' She sat up and stared sleepily at him, her mind clouded with sleep. 'I——'

'You cried out, just as I was passing your door,' Matt lied to her. He was inside her room now, closing the door, shutting them in together in a warm, dark tomb of intimacy that made her stomach muscles quiver.

'I suppose it's Travis and Gracie,' she heard Matt saying gently. 'I suppose I should have expected this. Poor Emily...I know just how it feels.'

Who had given him permission to sit on her bed? He was, she recognised, on his way to his bedroom from the bathroom because he was wearing a bathrobe and, she suspected, very little else. She could smell the fresh male scent of his soap and see the dampness of his hair.

'Come on. Have a good cry if you want to,' he offered comfortingly, and, before she could say a word, he had practically lifted her out of bed and tucked her along his side, so that she was nestled against him and his arms were around her.

'Mm...this is nice,' he commented appreciatively, touching the pretty lace that edged the bodice of her nightdress. 'This is the colour you should have for your wedding dress—sort of ivory. It suits you.'

Maybe it did, but surely that was no reason for his index finger to suddenly start tracing the delicate edging of the lace where it dipped over her breasts?

'Yes, it's very nice,' he murmured, and suddenly Emily had the conviction that he was not referring to the lace any more.

This really was dangerous. She must tell him to go. She tried to do so, but her vocal cords seemed to be paralysed. So did her hands, because they made no attempt whatsoever to remove Matt's when they gently pushed down the straps of her nightdress, so that the bodice fell away from her, completely revealing her breasts.

She did manage to find her voice then, protesting huskily, 'Matt.'

But he ignored her, saying softly, 'It's so much more comfortable like this, isn't it, Emily? Don't worry. I know you love Travis, and I completely respect your feelings; after all, it isn't as though it's the first time we've slept together, is it?'

Slept together. Matt intended sleeping here, with her. She couldn't let him do that, but, instead of telling him as much, Emily discovered that she was weakly and wantonly allowing him to gently tuck her beneath the covers, and to join her there—and without the towelling robe he had been wearing when he came into her room.

'Mm...this *is* nice, isn't it?' he murmured as he drew her slowly against him.

Nice wasn't the description she would have chosen, Emily thought dizzily. Wonderful, dangerous, mind-bogglingly desirable, yes—but nice?

'Mm...there's something just right about the way you feel in my arms Emily, do you know that? You're still too far away, though.'

Too far away! Any closer and she'd be... She swallowed nervously as Matt ignored her rigid tension and closed the small space between them by wriggling close to her.

'Mm...yes, you do feel good.'

Good. On the contrary, she felt far from good. 'Matt,' she protested a second time.

He lifted his head and looked down at her, and, if that small movement somehow meant that every inch of his skin where it met hers dragged ever so gently and erotically against her in a way that made her tremble with arousal and need, she prayed that only she was aware of it.

'I'm sorry, Emily, don't ask me to make love to you. I can't, not knowing that you love another man.'

Emily was lost for words. Don't ask him? A fierce thrill of anger ran through her. How dared he assume? She had had no intention of doing any such thing. Ask him to make love to her, indeed. She took a deep breath and then another and then discovered that the gentle friction of her naked breasts against his chest had stimulated them to such an extent that they actually seemed to be quite wantonly pushing against the solid wall of muscle, as though deliberately trying to incite a response from him.

Apprehension weakened her anger. She tried discreetly to pull away from him, and when she couldn't move said breathlessly, 'Matt, it would help if you didn't hold me quite so closely. I know you only want to help but——'

She tried to wriggle free and froze as she discovered the effect that movement had on her rebellious body. 'Matt,' she demanded.

'Just lie still and go to sleep. You'll feel better in the morning.'

Better? Did he really not know what he was doing to her? Of all the stupid, insensitive, thoughtless creatures. Emily seethed bitterly, knowing that the only way she was ever going to feel any better was if she stopped breathing.

She was desperate enough to even try doing that, holding her breath until she couldn't hold it any longer, and then letting it leak slowly out of her lungs, but somehow or other during the short space of time she had been holding it Matt had closed the tiny distance he had managed to create between them. He had also somehow or other managed to fall asleep, as well, she realised indignantly as she listened to his even, undisturbed breathing and fought against the sensual messages sent to her brain by her rebellious body.

She appreciated that Matt was acting out of the kindest of motives, she acknowledged frustratedly, but really she would far rather he had simply just walked on past her door. Either that or that he would wake up and...

And what? Make love to her? She shuddered as she acknowledged the impossibility of what she was thinking. The trouble was that, while her brain and her heart had no difficulty at all in accepting that while she might love *him*, Matt most certainly did not love her, her body seemed to have erected an impenetrable barrier against this knowledge and defied all her attempts to convince it that its wanton desire for Matt no longer seemed to be reciprocated.

How ironic *that* was.

All that panic when Matt had first arrived here, all the problems which had now arisen from her defensive lies about being engaged, all her self-contempt and soul-searching anguish on believing that Matt wanted to establish a relationship with her which was based merely on sex—and now here she was lying naked at his side, aching for him to wake up and make love to her, while he...

She heaved a deep sigh and forced herself to turn round so that she was lying with her back to him; she even managed to lift and remove his heavy arm from around her waist. After all, if he could sleep then so, surely, could she.

Only every time she managed to establish a small distance between them, Matt would either move in his sleep so that he was lying just as close to her as he had originally been, or, even worse, when she rebelliously decided to move away from him altogether, his arm came out and curled around her waist, drawing her back against him. And there *was* something blissfully pleasurable about sleeping within the curve of his body, absorbing its heat, lulled to sleep by his heartbeat, she acknowledged drowsily.

Only when he was sure that she was actually asleep did Matt dare to open his eyes, ruefully wondering if his plan wasn't far more likely to backfire on him than coax Emily into admitting that she loved him.

It was much later than usual when Emily woke up. She could tell that by the angle of the sun glinting through her window. She had slept much more deeply than usual, much more relaxingly. She stretched her body luxuriously and then froze.

'Mmm, I wondered when you were going to wake up, sleepyhead,' Matt murmured softly in her ear. He started nuzzling her throat, teasing the soft flesh behind her ear, making her come sharply awake.

'Matt,' she protested, and then froze a second time as her bedroom door opened and Gracie came in carrying a tray with two mugs of coffee on it.

'So,' she teased, putting them down beside the bed. 'It's just as well Uncle John *didn't* come home last night, isn't it, you naughty things?'

Emily knew she had gone bright pink from head to foot. The amusement dancing in Gracie's eyes made it obvious that her sister thought they had spent the night making love. She remembered how last night she had planned to take Gracie on one side this morning and confess to her what she had done, to beg her for her help, to tell her that Matt meant nothing to her.

'Travis and I will be going out in half an hour or so. We won't be back until dinnertime. Is there anything we can get for you while we're in Oxford, Emmy?'

Emily wanted to beg her to stay—she needed to unburden herself to her, but Gracie was already heading for the door and she could scarcely leap out of bed in her unclad state and run after her. And how was she going to convince Gracie that Matt meant nothing to her, that she did not want this engagement, that she felt nothing for him, when her sister had seen her in bed with him with her own two eyes?

Her expression betrayed far more than she knew as she watched the door close behind her sister, but Matt refused to allow himself to weaken.

There was only one thing for it now, Emily decided tiredly. She would have to tell *Matt* the truth—or at least some of it, she decided cautiously. She *couldn't* tell him that she loved him. That would have to remain her secret. No, but she *could* tell him that she had lied about Travis, and why.

She took a deep breath and said quickly, 'Matt, there's something I have to tell you.'

She focused on him and saw that he was looking gravely back at her. The overnight growth of his beard had darkened his jaw, and she ached to reach out and touch it . . . to reach out and touch *him*.

She was shaking inside, terrified by what she had to do, but she had to bring an end to this farcical engagement before things went any further. Soon Uncle John would be back—this might be her only real chance to talk properly to Matt.

She took another deep breath, and discovered that Matt had taken hold of one of her hands under the bedclothes, and that he was holding it almost comfortingly, as though he knew what she was going through and was trying to help her.

That feeling, ridiculous and unfounded though it was, gave her the courage to say breathlessly, 'Matt, I lied to you. I have never been engaged to Travis, nor to anyone else.'

She waited anxiously for him to betray the anger she knew he must be feeling, the explanations he was sure to demand, but instead, astoundingly, his grip on her own hand tightened slightly and he said simply, 'Yes, I know.'

'You *know*!'

Suddenly *she* was the one who was angry. She pulled away from him and tried to sit up, realising only when the bedclothes slid off her body revealing her breasts just how inappropriate such an action was.

There was something extremely difficult about being angry with another person when you were virtually lying in their arms, when they were looking at you with a grave concentration that made your heart ache, and when there was nothing you really wanted to do more than to lean over and kiss the male mouth so temptingly close to your own, Emily acknowledged dizzily.

'But you can't know,' she protested weakly. And then another thought struck her. 'But if you know, then why did you pretend that we were engaged? I——'

'No. Your explanations first,' Matt interrupted her quietly.

Her explanations first. Emily looked uncertainly at him. He looked very determined, stern almost, and yet behind that sternness she was sure she could see anxiety, even pain, shadowing his eyes. Telling herself she was imagining it and acknowledging that he probably had every right to demand some kind of explanation from her, she steeled herself to be as honest with him as she could without revealing to him how she really felt about him.

'Come on, Emily,' he pressed determinedly. 'You were going to tell me why you pretended you were engaged to Travis.'

'Well...it was the shock of seeing you here,' she began shakily. 'And it *was* a shock. I thought——'

'That I'd demand that you make an honest man of me, and so to stop me you invented a non-existent fiancé,' Matt suggested roughly.

Emily gaped at him, unable to stop herself shaking her head and saying immediately, 'No— no, of course not.'

Was she really imagining that slight relaxation in the grimness round Matt's mouth?

'Well, if that wasn't the reason, then why *did* you appropriate your sister's fiancé?'

In view of what he had just said, the truth seemed so appallingly insulting that Emily wasn't sure how she was going to voice it. It had seemed perfectly logical then, when she didn't really know Matt, to assume that he, like Gerry, was quite prepared to use a woman sexually without feeling the slightest degree of emotion or commitment for her. Now that she actually knew Matt... She swallowed, wishing that this were all just a dream and that she would wake up and find herself... Where? Somewhere where Matt didn't exist? No, of course not. Even here, now, when her mind was stricken with guilt and pain, her body was drawing pleasure and comfort from its closeness to Matt's. Her body had no conscience, no doubts, no fears, she decided tiredly. It only knew that it loved Matt, while her heart, her mind, her brain...

'Why, Emily?' Matt prodded impatiently.

'I thought you were going to try to make me— I thought you wanted——'

Heavens, this was even more difficult than she had imagined. The words just stuck in her throat, refusing to be uttered, until Matt said evenly, 'You thought I wanted to make love to you, is that it?'

'Not exactly,' Emily told him quietly. 'I've already tried to tell you—I thought you wanted to have sex with me, Matt,' she told him, stressing the words with a distaste she couldn't quite hide. 'I thought you'd assumed because of—of what had already happened, that I'd be only too willing to be your sexual partner.'

He *was* angry now. She could see it in his eyes, in the tightening of his jaw and the small muscle that flickered dangerously there.

'You thought that——'

'I didn't know you, Matt,' she reminded him huskily.

'No, you didn't, so why assume that I would behave so—so basely? Did our lovemaking really mean so little to you, that you could actually think——' He broke off, so obviously angry and trying to control that anger that Emily felt her guilt increase.

'I'm sorry. I know I misjudged you, but everything you said seemed to confirm my fears. You said you wanted——'

'I said I wanted *you*, and I *did*, but never in the kind of cold-blooded, cynical way you're implying. *You* don't have much of an opinion of my sex, Emily, or is it just me?'

She shook her head, stopping him. 'No, it isn't you. On the contrary. The first time we met, you gave me the impression that *you* didn't have a very good opinion of *my* sex, Matt. My experience with men is—was very limited. I fell in love when I was at university, and he—Gerry—well, I thought he loved me in return, but he was just using me. He made it more than plain to me that for men sex is just a physical appetite, completely divorced from emotion.'

'For *some* men,' Matt corrected her, 'and for some *women*, too. Jolie, my fiancée, was the same. She was sleeping with me, letting me believe she loved me, when in reality...'

'She must have hurt you badly,' Emily whispered.

'I thought she did,' Matt murmured back, 'and, like a fool, I clung on to my resentment telling myself that no one was ever going to hurt me like that again. That I was never going to fall in love again.'

For no reason at all the timbre of his voice, the way he was looking at her, made Emily's heart jump frantically.

'Matt, I want——'

To get dressed, she had been about to say, but Matt stopped her before she got any further by interrupting softly, 'Mm...so do I. Last night was the closest I hope I ever come to hell. Sleeping next to you, wanting you, remembering—but first there's something very important which you and I have to sort out, and let me tell you, Emily Blacklaw, that this time I am not prepared to let you take advantage of me sexually until we *have* sorted it out.'

Emily stared at him. 'Matt——'

'No,' he insisted virtuously. 'I mean it, Emily. No matter how much I want to make love to you, no matter how much you make me ache, no matter how crazy it's been driving me knowing that I was your first lover and wanting to be your only lover, I am not prepared to let you use me for sexual satisfaction. Not unless you're prepared to make both an emotional and a legal commitment to me.'

Emily wondered if she dared actually believe what she was hearing. Beneath the bedclothes Matt's hands were stroking her skin, doing all manner of distracting things to her senses, turning her weak with need and longings. 'Matt,' she murmured dizzily.

'I'm tired of playing games, Emily. Tell me that this thing between us means as much to you as it does to me, tell me you want me . . . tell me you love me.'

Immediately she tensed, searching his face warily, wondering how on earth he knew, and why he was choosing this particular method to inform her of that knowledge.

'Emily, please! I can't go on like this much longer. It's driving me out of my mind. *You're* driving me out of my mind. All these weeks of living close to you, wanting you, believing you belonged to someone else, and wanting to kill him for not

looking after you, for not loving you as he ought...
I couldn't understand *why* you had needed to turn
to me for physical satisfaction—for physical love.
I couldn't understand *why* he had not valued and
treasured the precious gift you gave to *me*. All these
weeks and I haven't known whom I hated the most,
him for having your love, you for loving him and
not me, or myself for loving a woman I couldn't
have. When I discovered the truth—when I found
out yesterday from Gracie that Travis was never engaged to you, I told myself you deserved to be pun-
ished for what you've put me through. I told myself
that, since I already knew you wanted me physically, somehow or other there must be a way I could
teach you to want me emotionally as well, but I
can't go on with it. Another ten seconds in this
damn bed with you in my arms like this, and I'm
going to forget everything I've told myself and make
love to you, and that's the last thing I should be
doing if you don't love me as I love you, if there's
no future in what I feel for you, if all you were
really doing the night we met was indulging in some
sexual exploration.

'So be honest with me now, Emily, for both our
sakes. Either you love me and want me as I do you,
or you don't.'

Emily swallowed hard. If every word he had just
spoken to her hadn't been raw with emotion and
truth, just one look into his eyes would have convinced her that this was no game, no clever deceit.
Her throat ached so much she couldn't speak,
couldn't tell him what was in her heart, couldn't
do anything other than place her head on his
shoulder and kiss the rigid outline of his throat,

tenderly at first and then less gently as she felt his involuntary reaction to her caress.

'Stop that, you witch,' she heard him growl, his fingers sliding almost roughly into her hair as he tilted her head back so that he could look into her face. 'I meant what I said, Emily,' he told her hoarsely. 'I won't...I *can't* make love to you without a commitment from you, without knowing that you share what I feel for you.'

'Oh, Matt, you must know I love you. I've betrayed it a thousand times. Every time I'm with you. I couldn't bear it—loving you, knowing you so intimately. I don't know how it happened, but that first night——'

'Without either of us knowing it emotionally or intellectually, we fell in love,' Matt finished for her. 'Our bodies, our senses were wiser than our minds. *They* knew what our intellects refused to acknowledge. We fell in love the night we met, Emily. Since then we've both done everything we can to confuse things. Both of us have clung on to our bad memories and used them as barriers against the truth, to deny our real feelings and to try to destroy our love. It hasn't worked, and now I think the time has come for us both to acknowledge the truth. We love one another. I want that love to flourish and grow, Emily. I want to marry you, give you children, share a lifetime with you—nothing else will be enough.'

'I feel the same way, Matt. For weeks after I left you I kept on hoping——'

'I tried to trace you, through your car, but you'd had it transported down here, and giving me a fictitious name didn't help, either. I hadn't given up, though, Emily, I promise you that. I was just waiting to get settled down here before I started combing every village, every farm along that road to find out where you'd come from—and I would have found you too, if fate hadn't decided to intervene. *She* obviously didn't have a very high opinion of either of us, did she?'

He cupped her face and kissed her tenderly, and then far less tenderly, breaking away from her eventually despite her soft protest.

'No, my love, I'm afraid we can't make love,' he whispered back to her. 'That first time we were lucky, but it would be tempting fate a little too much to rely on that luck a second time round. It won't be long, though. We will marry in June, and I think your Uncle John will be quite happy to sell this place to us and move closer to the university.'

'He could always stay here. There's plenty of room.'

'Oh, no. I'm not having my wife turned into a slave. I'm very fond of the old man, but I resent the way he treats you sometimes. I *know* you enjoy your domesticity, but my view is that it's something that should be shared, not something to which a woman is relegated—and besides, I shall want you to myself for a very, very long time. There's an awful lot of work for you to do in that garden yet,' he added teasingly.

Emily had stopped listening. She was too busy discovering the pleasure of tasting the strong, warm male body so temptingly close to her own, rediscovering the magic of that one very special night they had shared, in allowing herself to revel in the knowledge that Matt returned her love.

* * *

'Emily, you're looking marvellous. When is the baby due?'

'Another two months yet,' Emily responded, beaming at Matt as he stood proudly at her side. It was almost a year since they had married, and now it was Gracie's and Travis's turn.

Her aunt was saying something, asking them if they were permanently settled in Oxford, and once she had gone Matt bent his head and muttered to her, 'Don't think I don't know why you're looking so pleased with yourself, Mrs Slater. That little bundle of joy you've got tucked away in there has very effectively put an end to your enforced labours in the garden, and don't think I don't realise it.'

Emily grinned at him and teased back, 'Ah, but don't forget that you had rather a lot to do with this bundle of joy, as you call it. An awful lot, as I seem to recall.'

'Mm . . . are you sure Dr Jacobs thinks it might be twins?'

'She swears it is. Do you mind?'

'Not if you don't.'

'The only thing that I mind is that we wasted all that time before discovering that we loved one another.'

'Mm . . . and whose fault was that?'

On the other side of the room, Gracie grinned at her husband and said, 'Will you look at those two? *We're* the newlyweds, not them. They're an old married couple now.'

'Yes, well, my guess is that Matt's making the most of it before she gets any bigger and he can't get his arms round her!' Travis returned wryly.

Oblivious to the interest they were causing, Emily and Matt stayed locked in one another's arms, sharing a lingering lovers' kiss, the rest of the world forgotten.

1992

Celebrate the most romantic day of the year with
MY VALENTINE 1992—a sexy new collection of four
romantic stories written by our famous Temptation
authors:

> GINA WILKENS
> KRISTINE ROLOFSON
> JOANN ROSS
> VICKI LEWIS THOMPSON

My Valentine 1992—an exquisite escape into a romantic
and sensuous world.

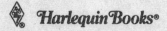

Harlequin Books®

HARLEQUIN *Temptation*

Rebels & Rogues

All men are not created equal. Some are rough around the edges. Tough-minded but tenderhearted. Incredibly sexy. The tempting fulfillment of every woman's fantasy.

When it's time to fight for what they believe in, to win that special woman, our Rebels and Rogues are heroes at heart.

Josh: He swore never to play the hero ... unless the price was right.

THE PRIVATE EYE by Jayne Ann Krentz.
Temptation #377, January 1992.

Matt: A hard man to forget ... and an even harder man not to love.

THE HOOD by Carin Rafferty.
Temptation #381, February 1992.

At Temptation, 1992 is the Year of Rebels and Rogues. Look for twelve exciting stories about bold and courageous men, one each month. Don't miss upcoming books from your favorite authors, including Candace Schuler, JoAnn Ross and Janice Kaiser.

Available wherever Harlequin books are sold. RR-1

HARLEQUIN
PROUDLY PRESENTS
A DAZZLING NEW CONCEPT IN ROMANCE FICTION

One small town—twelve terrific love stories

Welcome to Tyler, Wisconsin—a town full of people
you'll enjoy getting to know, memorable friends and
unforgettable lovers, and a long-buried secret that
lurks beneath its serene surface....

JOIN US FOR A YEAR IN THE LIFE OF TYLER

Each book set in Tyler is a self-contained love story;
together, the twelve novels stitch the fabric of a
community.

LOSE YOUR HEART TO TYLER!

The excitement begins in March 1992, with
WHIRLWIND, by Nancy Martin. When lively, brash
Liza Baron arrives home unexpectedly, she moves
into the old family lodge, where the silent and
mysterious Cliff Forrester has been living in seclusion
for years....

WATCH FOR ALL TWELVE BOOKS
OF THE TYLER SERIES
Available wherever Harlequin books are sold

TYLER-G